The
Cursed Empire
Waterbringer Unbound Book 2
By
T.C. Elofson

For Leanna

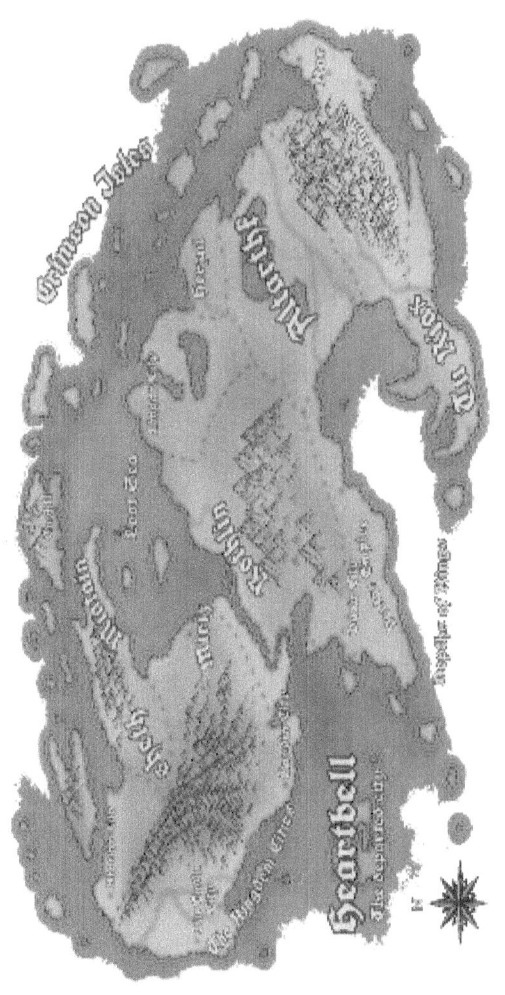

Crimson Isles
Rivedge
du Mox
Robbn
Heartbell
The Separated City

T he wind howled.

The snow was a sheet of white before Lady Cobalt. They hiked in solitude for many hours, moving down a steep gorge as her falcon watched the sun travel across the sky. Lady Cobalt's bird was an animal that chose to be air born on most sunrises in the snow. She could only guess that the bird loved mornings. Of course, Lady Cobalt had no evidence to support this claim, but she was sure she knew Igrit as well as any.

This high in the mountains, the winter storms, and the snow fog had blocked out the eye of the sun for many years, and the Vale kept the sun's rays from hitting the village in the summer and fall. Lady Cobalt hadn't felt warmth like it before and attempted to pull some of her furs off around her shoulders.

"Lady Cobalt, what are you doing?" Mika asked with a hint of a smile. "Don't tell me that this mere morning sun is too much for your mountain flesh to handle."

"Enough of you, old man," Cobalt sneered at him, a hint of a smile on her lips.

"Oh sure," said Mika, smiling at Cobalt, who walked beside him. It was the first sign of friendliness he had shown her. She didn't know what to think about the old Shinto-Kamie. If you asked Lady Cobalt a month ago, what she thought of the strange order called the Shinto-Kamie, she didn't know what she might say. The Shinto-Kamie Order was full of Reflections. Some were Mentalists, just like Lady Cobalt. But they didn't use the third sight. They didn't volunteer to lose their vision and give in to the sight like the Shadou-wāgu. However, besides all of that, she liked the older man. His way about him made it difficult for Cobalt to resist. She tried to keep her distance, but Lady Cobalt found it had to stay away as the days grew to weeks. And when he gave her the animal skin to wear, she liked him, the boy too.

Lady Cobalt drew near Roa and tugged up on his fears, sinching it around his neck.

"Thank you," Roa said, pulling off the rest of the giant wolf pelt that he wore around his small shoulders.

"I don't understand wearing pelts," Cobalt said. "The Shadou-wāgu never wear skins or furs over their flesh."

"How do you not simply freeze to death then?" Mika asked.

"The Shadou-wāgu are Mentalists. We have complete control over our minds. We can control our fear. We can suppress pain and take away the sting of the cold."

"Yet you cannot see without looking through *my* eyes," Mika said frostily.

"Does that thought unnerve you, Shinto-Kamie?"

"A little," he said with a laugh.

After that, the three fell silent again, and Roa watched the early morning fields come and go as they moved noiselessly through the brush. The ice of the frozen water lessened as the sun rose over the mountain peaks, and its warmth washed over the lake. The ice melted, and snow turned to water. With every step that Lady Cobalt took away from the cold of the mountains, the sky grew brighter and brighter.

This is what she loved, Lady Cobalt thought. She recalled the brightness in the sky, but it had been so long since she had felt the sun on her face, so long since she felt the heat in her flesh.

The narrow, sloping trail they climbed down some time later led to a vantage point in the countryside. From there, they could take in the landscape to the horizon. It was the first panoramic view that Lady Cobalt had witnessed in many years. But her falcone told her not to move too close to the trail's edge, for the slope down was severe, and the sharp rocks below could rip clear to the bone.

"How far down is that?" Roa asked Mika as he peered over the edge, fighting vertigo.

"Not too far of a drop, but those jagged teeth of granite would eat right through whatever flesh you had."

They stood there for a few minutes, and Lady Cobalt listened to the two converse about how much farther and other things. Lady Cobalt lost interest as her falcon swooped lower, taking up rest on her shoulder.

"Really?" Lady Cobalt said, reaching up to scratch under the small bird's chin. "Lazy bird."

"The Temple," Lady Cobalt heard Roa say suddenly. "What about the temple, Master Mika?" Roa asked. "You said it was your life's work."

"Aye, I did. Well, you know what they say, my boy. If it is meant to be, all roads will eventually lead you there. I think someone will find the answers even if I do not. Today I am with you, and this is more pressing."

"Thank you, Mika."

Lady Cobalt thought about the temple she first encountered, the Shinto-Kamie and Roa. They were studying the temple, going over the ancient texts, trying to understand the gods, to know them better. Lady Cobalt didn't understand that part. If she wanted to understand the gods, she would just ask them. They love to talk. Some gods never shut up, she thought.

The morning was gusty and cold, damp and miserable, yet. Then off in the distance, he saw them. Three riders approached on horseback, riding in from across rolling hills with the sun on their backs.

"Someone's coming, I think," Roa announced to Mika, who, so far, hadn't noticed the men on the large animals loudly plodding over the hills.

"What?" Mika's face transformed, suddenly serious with alarm. "Where?"

"Over there," Lady Cobalt thrust a finger in the direction of the riders. Mika stopped and looked intently across the field at the three men on black and brown horses.

"Riders," Cobalt said warily.

An arrow shot out of the morning fog at once and took Mika in the ribs. The long shaft dropped him, and he fell with a grunt. But as Roa tried to reach for him, Lady Cobalt's grasp fired at him, seizing his coat and ripping him backward. Several more arrow shafts pierced the ground around Lady Cobalt.

"No! Get back," she yelled as she tossed him to the snowy grass. She threw her body over his as arrows rained down around them. Long shafts thundered around them like the heavy rainfall drumming the soil. Lady Cobalt hugged Roa as best she could.

"We have to get back!" Mika hissed.

"I can't risk an arrow finding him." Lady Cobalt felt Roa trying to move, to squeeze out of her grasp. "No, Roa, don't. I will protect you."

Suddenly, Lady Cobalt felt a heat, an unbearable heat. In the cold night air, the heat overtook her. She felt a wetness at her back, a piercing inside her muscles. She couldn't move. The arrow in her back held her in place.

"I'm sorry, Roa," the words slipped from her. Pain washed over her, and the third arrow took her between the shoulder blades. She gave a little grunt and slumped on top of Roa.

"Lady Cobalt," Roa called for her. Lady Cobalt tried to respond. There was nothing. She never felt the last arrow—only the cold of the snow.

She heard everything. She heard Roa's sobbing. She listened to the footsteps around her. She heard the arrow that took Mika. But worst of all, Lady Cobalt heard when they pulled Roa free over her, there was nothing she could do to stop it.

"Mika!" Roa cried back to the sound of the Shinto-Kamie's voice. But Lady Cobalt heard no reply. The last words she heard were the words of her nightmares.

"We have him! We have the Soulchemist!"

The Archway loomed overhead. This is it, Takayo thought as she stared into the solid slab of stone buried in white powder. This doorway changed her life—the secret doorway between herself and Roa.

Takayo didn't know it when she sat in the rowboat on the dock. And when she gazed up at the sight of the mountains, it did not occur to her that she would be standing before the door she betrayed. She did betray it. The secret message she gave to the Gos Commander, the words to say that was the key to this door.

"On the other side is the temple?" Takayo asked. "What will the others do while we are in here?"

"They will go to Shi and report what happened to the council. We will meet Master Mika, who should be at the temple with Roa, the Soulchemist boy. He will translate the text for you. We will meet the order at the Port of Shi in three days. We must get the Soulchemist to safety."

"And what if they are not at the temple? What if they are dead? What if I killed them?"

"You didn't kill them," Master Kon reeled around on her. "Shihan killed them."

"My action could have killed them."

"No."

Takayo watched as Master Kon kneeled to the archway, pushing his mouth close to the rock. His voice was low, almost a whisper, as he said the words. Emotion rose inside Takayo as the rock shook and rumbled as it slid to the side, shaking mounds of fresh snow free, raining down at Master Kon's feet.

It took work for Takayo to walk mindlessly through the snow. Kon decided where and when to hike, and it was frustrating for Takayo, not knowing what turn they would take and where that turn might take them. Her fingers were numb by the first of their turns, and her toes were cold from her first step off the dock and into this horrible snow. Master Kon pushed them hard, moving at a brisk pace. It was far too fast for Takayo to hike and certainly too fast for Jon, who moved slowly, whimpering at the rear of their little party.

Takayo looked back at him, giving the boy the best smile she could manage under the circumstances, which wasn't all that great. But he smiled back at her just the same, a grin that said to her that there was not a winter wind that the gods had conceived of that might take Jon Rainwater's spirit away.

Master Kon moved them up a steep incline in a switchback trail up the east bank of what he called The Gods' Snake—a slick embankment that was half ice and half rock. Most of Takayo's steps fell upon the ice that threatened to send her reeling backward into Jon, who struggled just as badly as she did. Master Kon seemed to move like a mountain lion, stepping this way and that way, moving to this rock and then to another one. But when Takayo stepped upon the same stone as the old sword master, she slid backward.

"You step too lightly, Takayo," he finally told her, snatching her hand on one of her falls. "Stick the landing with the ball of your foot and grip with your toes."

He demonstrated, sending his toes slapping down at the ice. Yet when Takayo tried it, she slid, but not as severely.

As Takayo snatched one of the branches of a tree on the side of the path and pulled herself up, she found Master Kon examining it. He kneeled in the snow, looking very closely at where the base of the tree and the powder met.

"What is it?" she asked, brushing handfuls of snow from her furs.

"A cut on the tree. No more than three days old."

"Okay? So what about it?"

"Master Mika cuts trees as a marker for the order to find him."

"Okay...?"

"But he was in hiding. He wouldn't have done it unless he wanted someone to know where he was."

"I don't understand," Takayo said, walking closer to the tree. "Then why would he do it?"

"It doesn't make sense. His trail is heading *away* from the temple. The Order had intelligence that Master Mika and the Soulchemist were heading *to* the temple, but these tracks are clear—he is heading away."

"You think he's in trouble?" Jon said.

"Maybe. But I don't know for sure. We need to keep going. But keep an eye out for cuts in the trees."

"Of course, he's in trouble," Takayo said. "I sold the secret information for the Bushi to find the Soulchemist, right?"

"You can't blame yourself, Takayo," Master Kon said.

"Of course, I can blame myself. I put that boy in danger. I put your friend in danger too."

"The faster we get to the temple, the faster we will know if they are safe, okay?" Master Kon told her.

"Right."

For the next several hours, they walked slower than before. Master Kon moved them in a sort of zigzag pattern, monitoring the ground, the trees, and the rocks the whole time. Takayo watched him move, and even though she couldn't see the concern on Master Kon's face, she could feel it coursing through him. It seemed to her that his movements grew stiff with worry the farther they traveled. His steps were unsure when before they had been quick and pointed. Suddenly he grew rigid and stiff as a slab of ice.

"What is it?" she called to him as she and Jon ran up to him. He didn't say a word, but she followed his gaze. And when she saw it, too, she understood.

Blood. There was blood on the ground. Takayo thought that she knew who the blood belonged to... Yet she still hoped it wasn't Mika's.

K anon preferred to look out the large window over his feathered bed. It faced west and opened out to the sea. But when he thought of looking for a window to peer from that night, there would be no sign of the black water he searched for. There would be no sign of anything again, at least not for Kanon.

When he awoke, the smell of blood was in the air, full of acrid aromas. The tiny footfalls of a dog moved around him, and from time to time, a whimper pierced the air. Kanon found that his skull and face hurt when he tried to move. He couldn't recall why or what he had done the night before or the nights before. In fact, Kanon could scarcely remember the last few nights at all. Was it drink? He thought. He was one to enjoy ale, but in all his years of drinking, he could scarcely recall a time when the drink stole his memories.

Birds sang somewhere outside—he could hear them easily enough—but he could see no light. Not a single sun ray, yet it was warm inside his room under the heap of furs and blankets that covered him.

He was perspiring.

Sickly heat, Kanon thought groggily. *Ash and Embers, what in the gods happened to me?*

He felt fragile, and pain stabbed him when he touched his face. He moved his fumbling fingers up to his eyes, which felt odd. Blood was dried and flaked to the touch. That was strange to Kanon but not as bizarre as the crude stitching threaded through his closed eyelids and over the bridge of his nose. His head felt as if it weighed twenty pounds. It felt too heavy to lift it off his pillow. As for his body, he could barely feel his limbs at all. He had no memory of getting to his bed. He desperately racked his brain for answers but found none.

"What...?" The word stumbled from his mouth.

"Awake, are you?" a voice said from the darkness. Kanon turned in the direction of the words.

"Who's there? Please, I don't know what's going on."

"You've been hurt, my young Prince," the voice of Old Akira said. Kanon was grateful to hear the voice of his old house teacher. She was sitting next to him.

"A...Akira? I don't—"

"Hush now, child," the old woman said. "You have a lot of the dragon in you just now. Your brain will be sluggish," she said from her chair while doing some needlework. He could hear her fingers moving. He listened to the dragging of the heavy string pulled through the fabric.

"Oh, Uzume... the dragon..." Kanon said, suddenly realizing he was drugged to ward off the pain.

Why would they drug me?

"What happened to me?"

"You can't remember? Well, it will come back to you soon enough, I think. We just need to get that pesky dragon out of you first."

"What do *you* know, old woman?" Kanon snapped, his voice as petulant as a child. It was the same voice he gave her when he was younger. He had liked the way she used to prattle on. Before. But not now. Now Kanon wanted straight talk from her.

"You know, that tone was somewhat passable when you were my charge. But now, I must say... I don't much care for it." The old woman returned to her needlework without another word. Kanon sat up, frustrated by his blindness and the dizzy feeling of the dragon swimming in his blood.

"Old Akira, please," he began in a soft tone. "I'm terrified. I don't know what happened. I have no memory. And my eyes... I can't see anything at all."

"I know, child. And I am so very sorry for that. Truly, I am."

He heard her place her work next to her chair, the two sowing needles clanging against one another.

"Your servant boy found you on the floor of the stables. You had been attacked."

"Attacked?" Kanon repeated the word.

"Yes, it seems that… well, you took a sword to the face. Really, my boy, that sword-playing business—"

"But my eyes?" he asked, turning to where he thought she was.

"The blade cut through both eyes. The Ishi healer was forced to sew them closed."

"Sew them closed?!" Kanon spat out the words.

"My sweet Prince, the healer had to, or else your face would never heal. The guides of Kampo are very clear in these matters. The eyes were gone long before that. I'm sorry to say."

Kanon ran his fingers over his eyelids sewn shut and felt the sloppy, thick threads of catgut that webbed over what used to be his vibrant blue eyes.

"Why can't I remember what happened?"

"In time, you will remember. You shall also learn to deal with this new situation with your sight," she told him.

"Situation with my sight? I'm blind! There is no situation!"

"Calm yourself, my boy," she said patiently, looking back down at her needlework next to her.

"Please go now, old woman. Or at least be quiet. I feel sleep creeping up on me again." That was a lie. Kanon hated the idea of more rest. What he truly desired at that moment was time to think or to remember.

"So it is with the dragon, my Prince. Sleep well. I will look in on you after," she said, pushing her frail body out of the thin wooden chair where she sat. Kanon could hear the creaking of the chair and pictured her arms quivering as always when she pushed her way out of the chair that sat close to his bedside.

The next time he woke, the shutters over his windows sat drawn closed, and Mouse-mat stood over him with a single candle illuminating the childlike features of his face. When he saw Kanon begin to push the covers down, the boy kneeled close to him and spoke.

"My Lord, how is your health?"

Kanon tried to speak, but the first few words tumbled from his lips, tripping on the dragon's tail.

"I have no eyes, Mouse-mat."

He raised a hand to his face and touched his closed lids. Every touch pained him as his fumbling fingers grazed a strange bandage that sat over his face. It appeared as if a bandage had been added to his face since the last time he had awoken. It was tight and wet. His fingers tapped at the moisture over his eyes.

"Master, you must be still," Mouse-mat whispered. "You are grievously hurt. Your eyes, they have leaked—"

"Leaked, Mouse-mat?"

"Yes, my Lord. You clawed at them in your sleep, so we needed to wrap your eyes." Mouse-mat fell silent momentarily, but Kanon could still feel the boy's gaze. "Are you thirsty?"

"Yes. I can't remember the last time I had any water."

He heard Mouse-mat shuffling around close to him and clattering a glass flask, then the trickling of water into a chalice.

Kanon didn't understand how or if it was an effect of the Dragon, but somehow he had a sense of the surrounding. He had dipped into Mouse-mat's mind before, but this was strange. Now, the boy's mind seemed so open to Kanon that he could see what Mouse-mat saw. Kanon knew that if he reached out with his arm, his fingers would find Mouse-mat. So he did, and Kanon's hard landed on the shoulder of the boy.

"Here, Master," the boy said, and Kanon felt the rim of glass at his lips as a cold stream of water spilled onto his parched tongue. It poured a slow trickle down his throat, and Kanon couldn't recall enjoying a sip of water so much in his entire life. He swallowed it with a scratchy throat, and then he tasted it. The dragon was in the water. It seemed that the dragon was to be his companion for one more dream as well, he thought as he drifted away. Mouse-mat's voice fumbled in his ears, and then even that was gone. *Blast that boy*, Kanon thought.

This time Kanon dreamt that he was running through a darkened tunnel somewhere. Rocks slipped under his foot as he moved close to a stone pillar. There were bodies strewn about the dusty floor, and a young girl moved away from him around a corner. Suddenly she turned and faced him.

"Master Kon, over here," she addressed him, urging him closer. This was confusing, Kanon thought as he dreamt, watching the girl from what felt like inside the eyes of Master Kon. Kanon looked down as his fingers found the wrapped grip of a long Shi-ken sword at his hip. He ran his fingers along the ripped and dirty threads of Master Kon's robes. Robes that Kanon had seen many times.

"There's a door," the girl told him urgently.

He awoke many hours later, thinking the blinds were open though no light found his eyes. All felt wrong to him. But could it ever feel right? He wondered.

Kanon was alone for the first time. Pushing back a heavy fur, he attempted to sit up, but the pain struck with hot fingers, sending his head back down to the pillow again. He thought the line of agony across his face wasn't the only part of it. A spot on his ribs throbbed with angry thundering as he breathed, and an ache ran up his arm to his neck when he tried to sit up.

Ash and embers, what happened to me?

Every moment of what happened seemed as strange to him as the dream when he thought back on it.

Then a shadowy face filled his consciousness. There was also a blade of straight steel.

The thought of it sent chills down his arms, but he forced himself to continue down this path, to hold onto it in his head.

This man tried to kill me, Kanon thought. He knew it to be true.

He pushed himself up again, ignoring the pain. In the obscurity of his blindness, he threw his legs over the side of the bed, knocking over a long iron candlestick that clattered to the ground, reeling off one of his bookends. It sent a stack of old novels tumbling to the floor. He heard his dog jump at the noise and turned to the sound of his Akita panting.

"Sorry, boy," he told the dog apologetically. Kanon reached out with searching fingers. After a moment, he felt the soft tangle of the fur of the dog's strong back at his side and the wet nose in his palm.

He smiled at the thought of his dog close by. He climbed from his bed, and the blackness in his mind whirled around him. Even this tiny effort sent swirls of pain swimming up his arm and over his face. He stumbled forward with his hands out, slowly swinging in front of his chest, hoping to feel whatever might be near. This was his room. He had walked its floor in the middle of the night during the darkest times, but this was different. He was completely blind.

Somehow he did it. He moved from the small space of his bed to the closed door, even moving around the small chest and dog bed. He stopped when needed and stepped over objects that he knew were there.

Though the room was dank and cold, his body burned with sickness.

Fever, he thought. But he didn't care.

He had dreamt of a stranger, of a sword that was odd to look at. He held the picture close in his mind of the stranger in the stables. His fingers groped and fumbled at the cold iron doorknob of his chamber door. After a few tries, he grabbed it and yanked his heavy door open. Cool air from the hall washed over his face, and the smell of lavender and sage danced up to him.

Suddenly footsteps sounded in the hall before him, and the cautious tones of Mouse-mat found him.

"Master, do you thirst? I have your water."

"No more of that water, boy," Kanon snapped from the doorway.

"You must not fight. Do not try to move much, my Lord. You need to rest."

"Rest," he laughed. "I've rested for days. No more rest, Mouse-mat. Now step aside!"

"Of course, I will do as my Master bids, to be sure. But, Lord Kanon, your wounds...."

"I've had enough of the dragon for one lifetime. Thank you, boy," he said, stepping from the doorway and down the hall, the whole time his hands held out and searching for the servant.

"Now help me down this hall."

"Yes, Master."

Kanon found a handful of silk—the shirt the boy wore—and held on to it. He barged in his blindness for several paces with Mouse-mat leading the way. He shuffled in the darkness around a corner, down another hall, and then around another corner. Strange how he knew every turn and corner of the White Palace in the seeing world, but in his blindness, he knew none of it.

"What is this?" the voice of the Ishi healer sounded in Kanon's darkness.

"Sir Healer," Mouse-mat said. "The Master insisted."

"Insisted on what, boy? Infecting his wounds?" the healer growled.

"I insisted on seeing my mother, Ishi. Now step out of our way. I have business with the Empress."

"Every moment you are out of bed puts you in greater danger, Prince Kanon."

"I am blind. What else can happen?" Kanon said, inching a little closer to the voice.

"The infection could poison your blood, Prince. And kill you. That bandage doesn't look good at all. I want to have a look at it."

Footsteps moved closer to Kanon, and he felt the man stand near him.

"If you must."

He felt rough fingers on his face. He thought about their work under the bandage, and it felt cool after a moment. The air hit the flesh where the bandage had been. There was also pain, but Kanon did his best to ignore it. The dressing came off entirely, and his skin felt wet under it. The Ishi discarded the bandage, still damp and crusty with blood.

"Be still, Master. The stitches must be washed."

The Ishi's touch was gentle, but the warm water sent pain flaring up like a fire. Kanon tried to picture what he must have looked like with the angry cut across his face and the stitching over his eyes.

What a sight this prince must be, he thought despondently.

And what of this Empress that was like a mother to him? What would she think of him now? This person only cared about impressions, status, and image. What would she feel about her adopted boy?

She will execute me for sure now, he thought with fear.

"This part will pain you some, my Lord," the healer warned.

At once, a warm liquid that stunk of alcohol washed over his eyes. It did more than pain him, sending long fingers of searing agony through his face and neck that felt like he was being burned alive. It traced a line of fire across the slice mark over Kanon's flesh.

"Ash and embers, man! Do you wish me dead?"

"Nearly done, my Prince," the healer said, dabbing at the stitches with the wet cloth. "It would be wise to replace the bandage, my Lord, until the stitching has healed a bit more. It still looks clean, though. We found you in the stable with the horse dung; your wounds were in filthy shape. Now it looks to be healing cleanly."

"Good. Can I go then?" Kanon asked, frustrated.

"A new bandage is necessary, my Lord."

He heard the Ishi root around somewhere nearby for several minutes before returning to him with a fresh roll of silk. The healer gently wrapped the bandage around Kanon's face and eyes. It was noticeably not as tight as before.

In the royal chambers, a single white raven was humming tunelessly as Kanon came through the door, led by Mouse-mat. When the bird spotted the Prince, it grew still and quiet. The Empress lounged in a grand armchair, covered in a heavy wrap and reading a book. With each turn of the page, Kanon pictured her there as he had seen her do on countless occasions in the past. Yet as he approached, he felt that odd sensation again that he could sense the room.

She looked up and spoke his name tiredly. "Kanon."

"So you do remember me then, Mother?" he said, inching closer to the sound of her voice. "I had begun to wonder."

"It's so perfect to see you up and moving," her voice tinged with irritation. "Though I confess I did not think I would see you in my rooms."

"If I were to wait for you... well, I would die of boredom."

"And what would you have me do, Kanon? I ordered you not to go out. The gods have struck you down for betraying the Empress of Hisan. There seems little left more me to do."

"The gods?!" he snapped in his blindness. "The gods didn't take my eyes! A swordsman all in black did with one cunning slice of a Chokuto blade. *He* took them!"

His words boomed in the darkness, but he heard their tone sink around him as he spoke.

"What swordsman?" her voice found him, sure and stern.

"I don't know. I have no memory of the attack. I—"

"No memory? Then how do you know it was a swordsman all in black?" she asked, standing up from her chair and slapping her book on a nearby table.

"I have a picture of the attacker in my mind. I would recognize him again if I saw him. If I *could* see him."

"See him? You are BLIND!"

"I know..."

"Yet you have no idea why you were attacked or why you were in the stables?" the Empress said, stepping closer to Kanon. "My boy, the dragon is a powerful drug—"

"No!" Kanon snapped. "Don't dismiss this as a drug-induced hallucination. Someone did this to me. I almost died. A sword nearly cut me in half. I fought this man. He was not trained in the art of the Bushi but in something else... Something foreign to me. I demand—"

"Okay... okay, my boy," The Empress said, placing small hands on his shoulders and trying to calm him. "I will see it done. I will investigate the matter and what comes of it."

"Thank you, Mother," Kanon said with a doubtful sigh. He felt the Empress lean forward and give him a soft kiss on the cheek, which he noted was not like her to do. His adopted mother was not someone that he associated with emotion or love by any means. He could recall only a handful of times when the Empress kissed him, and on each occasion, she was covering something up. This time pinged his curiosity as she returned to her chair and snatched her book off the side table.

"Back to bed with you now, boy. You still have some healing left to do, I think."

Kanon wished he had eyes to look at her with. He could always look upon her face and see the falseness within her, but now everything was blind to him. However, there was something within him that was sure there was something else, something sinister, that she was hiding from him.

"Let's go, Mouse-mat," Kanon said, turning toward the door. Just then, a figure entered the doorway, and Mouse-mat abruptly stopped.

"Oh, pardon me, Sir," Mouse-mat said, moving around the man.

"Out of my way, runt! Oh, Prince Kanon, I didn't see you there."

The voice was oddly familiar to him, but Kanon couldn't place it for some reason. The man moved past Kanon and Mouse-mat and entered the chambers, bowing stiffly before the Empress.

As Kanon walked around the corner, he abruptly halted. The sudden lack of movement was jarring to his servant, who tried to turn and speak, but Kanon muffled his words.

"Quiet, boy. I want to listen."

The two stood close to the open doorway of the Empress' chambers as the loud-mouthed man spoke to her.

"What is it, Commander?" the Empress asked sternly.

"The girl escaped with the help of Master Kon."

"Escaped?! How could she escape?" the Empress snapped at him.

"It was that Shinto-Kamie girl, the one who sold the information to me. She is very powerful."

"This minor Kamie you told me about, Commander... This girl killed the guards?" the Empress said, clearly angry now. "How could a low-born Reflection kill so many of your men?"

"This girl may have worn the robes of a minor Reflection, but she's an Elementalist and a very powerful one. She fooled me, and we lost them both. Both Kon and the girl. Please, Empress, forgive me. It is my doing. I—"

"I will deal with you later, Commander..." the Empress trailed off. "This girl must have been a Shinto-Kamie ploy to get the Master. Now the Order has both of them, and we have nothing!"

Kanon could hear the rage in her voice. He listened to the anger, and it pleased him a bit to know that she was frustrated. But his mind reeled at what had happened to Master Kon.

Is he really gone? Is the man who trained and raised me really gone? And for what?

"Rally your men, Commander."

"Yes, Empress!" The Commander bowed.

"I want them found and brought to me, dead or alive."

Kanon's thoughts ran rampant. Master Kon wasn't only his teacher; he was his friend.

Curse my blindness. Kanon urged Mouse-mat down the hall. Kanon heard the Commander leave the chambers behind him and felt relieved they had listened unseen.

"Mouse-mat," Kanon said. "We need to find out what happened to Master Kon, and I want to know everything you can find out about this girl."

"Yes, my Lord."

"Everything, is that understood, Mouse-mat?"

"Understood."

The blood on the pile of leaves was dark—almost black—but it was easy enough to see. It was blood, and it was a good amount. Not enough to take a life, but enough for Master Kon to have a look on his face that worried Takayo. Master Kon plucked a leaf in two fingers from the ground. He held it up in the light of the midnight moon.

"This wouldn't kill him," Master Kon said, turning the leaf over in his fingers. "Master Mika had a Reflection of healing. Almost any wound—except for losing his head—he would heal from. But I don't like the look of this. He was marking trees, and he was injured. This blood trail leads away from the temple. I really think—"

"The temple doesn't matter," Takayo said. "We can…

"NO! We cannot go against the gods. First the temple and then Mika."

Kon looked at her and then over to where Jon stood as if he was asking Jon's opinion on the matter.

"Understood. Let us hurry. How far do we have to go?" she asked, looking up the steep incline before her.

"Eight miles if we take this path. Four, if we go over rough terrain. However, I don't recommend that way."

"Why?" Jon asked.

"The Uenhal Mountains are twenty thousand meters straight up. The temple is on the base of the southwestern peak, which is a treacherous climb over ice, fallen trees, and sheer drop-offs. It's too dangerous. We will go a long way, but we need to hurry. There is an abandoned village at the base of the peak where we can rest. But until then, there will be no shelter and no place to stop."

"Understood, Master," Takayo said, giving Jon a look that said, 'Shut up and let us be off.'

No one could move quickly in the deep snow they walked in now. Master Kon stepped first, and Takayo stepped in his large tracks, trusting his judgment. Behind her, Jon followed her lead, stepping in her footprints. Takayo took notice of Master Kon's movements, and how he seemed not to breathe, or if he did, it was slight and silent. It was as if he listened to the mountain and didn't want his breath to distract him.

The sky they climbed toward turned orange to pink and then to blue. The mountain path bore signs of footsteps and deep impressions in the snow. The tracks had gone in some places, shallowly covered with new snow, but others told the tale enough. Master Mika had come through here.

Takayo moved as quickly as the deep snow would allow, but that wasn't fast. She moved, trudging, though stubbornly, pulling her fur boots out of Kon's deep steps.

"I like the snow and the winter," Jon told her in his childlike manner, and she laughed at his optimism.

"This isn't winter here, boy. This is fall. The winter will come soon enough, and very little will survive it," Master Kon told him. "Winter here is ferocious, like an angry tiger."

"Oh." Jon fell silent.

Takayo sucked in a great mouthful of cold water-air and let the elements fill her. Again her mind awoke, and her muscles strengthened, helping Takayo march through the ever-thickening snow before her. Jon seized her arm, seeing what she was up to, and she pulled him up the steep incline, nearly passing Master Kon in the process.

"Good, Takayo. Use the elements around you. Very good," Master Kon said as she moved close to him. She looked at him for a long moment and smiled. Master Kon had no Elemental ability, yet he quickly climbed the steep slopes of the mountains. He had no gifts to call upon the elements around him to strengthen his muscles, yet he pushed on. *How?* Takayo wondered.

The weather held the cold for many hours as they walked. They moved as fast as they could—as quickly as the rough terrain would allow—and arrived at the small but long abandoned village just before the sun began to set. As they turned the final corner around a rather fat and pudgy-looking oak, Takayo caught the first sign of the empty town. It was barely noticeable under the weight of so much powder and ice. The thin roof peaks just peered under the snow piles. Most of the wooden structures were inaccessible to them as they moved through the village, save for one. The first building on their right looked clear of compacted snow, but it did have a scattering of fresh powder on its wooden planks.

As Master Kon threw open the sodden wooden door, Takayo noticed how the shack looked lived in. Not that someone was currently living in it, but it looked like someone had recently used it as shelter. She watched as Master Kon moved around the room in his usual manner, looking for evidence or any sign that might bring him some hope. She watched as he moved to the small living space's far side and kneeled on the floor.

"What is it?" Jon asked from the doorway.

"Footprints. They were here."

"How long ago?" Takayo asked.

"Hard to tell. The impressions are closed off from the environment, but if I were to guess, I would say four days. The snowfall outside has been rather light, yet there are no tracks—"

"So because there are no tracks, you think it's been some time?" Takayo said.

"Right." Master Kon looked around the room again, a little more like someone looking over a campsite with the knowledge of bedding down for warmth. "We will be fine here for the night. We will head out in the morning for the temple."

"How much farther?" Jon asked, nearly exhausted and taking a seat on a clean spot on the floor. Master Kon knelt across from him and reached into his satchel.

"No more than four hours," he told them, pulling out a blanket.

"Four hours? Why are we stopping then?" Takayo insisted in a tone that she didn't like, but it was the most common tone with her, like a note on a flute. Like a bamboo flute, the insistent tone slipped out of her as it always did.

"Tonight we sleep. We don't know what we might find up there. Something happened to Master Mika and the Soulchemist. I want us rested and ready to handle anything tomorrow. As for you, girl," Master Kon shot her a look of irritation, "replenish your water. Whatever tests the gods have for you might drain you, so prepare yourself as well as possible."

"So what do we do now?" Jon asked and pulled food from his satchel.

"We eat, Jon. And sleep." Takayo watched Jon for a moment. He eyed his sad-looking food.

"Something wrong?" she asked.

"What? Oh, no... not really. I want something else. Like maybe a hare. I bet there are lots of rabbits in these hills, right, Master Kon?"

Kon eyed him briefly before answering as if he didn't want to admit the truth to Jon. "Yes, but if you want a rabbit, go get it yourself."

Takayo watched from her corner of the stone hearth an hour later as Jon worked a blazing fire. A freshly skinned and pink rabbit simmered on a stick over the long flames as he poked at several of the logs, and sparks danced up around the animal.

Jon's fresh kill roasting over the fire. That was something that had never occurred to her before—Jon was a boy of the woods. A boy is just as skilled at hunting as building fires. The smell of cooking meat made Takayo sad and melancholy. Her stomach rumbled louder than she would have liked as Jon tested the meat.

"Not long," he told her, smiling at her.

"Good."

The following day dawned crisply with a harsh winter-like wind that howled from the north. It brought a bitter cold whipping into the empty village. They set off headstrong into the chilly gust at first light. The four hours of rest was nothing after hunting and cooking the rabbit. Her muscles were weaker than she wanted, but going to sleep hungry had never worked out well for her.

Takayo pulled her furs tighter around her face and eyes, but large wet snowflakes pelted her and worked under the heavy folds of fur. Before long, the snow melted and soaked into the fabric close to her skin.

"I can't see," she yelled through the snowstorm as whiteness overtook the space around her. The cold seemed to attack her from all sides, including from below.

"Focus on the ground."

The wind viciously lashed at her face, and she attempted something she hadn't done before. Takayo tried to communicate with her second elemental power. She reached out with her mind and found the water that swirled around her quickly enough, but she saw no other element ready for her will.

"Why don't I just—"

"No! Takayo, don't. Save yourself for the temple," Master Kon snapped, returning to face her. "Just focus on the ground and stay behind me." He said that last part with a calming voice. "We don't have long to go."

They marched on for several minutes, heads down, as the wind roared past her ears. It wasn't until they had finally tucked down into a grove of trees that they found some shelter from the wind. They moved close to a rock wall slick with ice and skirted near it as they climbed what looked like stone steps. It was the first sign of any manufactured structure that Takayo had seen outside the buried village.

The steps were long and fat and covered with a coating of slick ice. Takayo nearly lost her balance on the first several steps, but Jon was there to brace her with a friendly hand. Frustrated, she looked up at Master Kon, who had slid to the side of the step instead of climbing in the center like Jon and Takayo. He moved with the skill of a well-practiced dancer, progressing with ease.

When am I going to learn? Takayo scolded herself silently and followed suit.

She moved up the long staircase in the ice flanked by hulking trees and looming rock walls. When she finally spotted the temple, she had to admit that it didn't look like much. Even though several of the pillars had been recently cleaned off, they still looked like something forgotten in time.

Long fractured pillars shot from the confines of the snow like tall trees reaching up to the sun. They stood white and smooth, displaying their finely crafted marble as she moved closer. Takayo stepped between the two closest pillars and braced herself, grabbing them with her hands. Clumps of snow fell over the tops of her fingers as she moved her hands over the sides of the pillars.

"This is it, Takayo," Master Kon told her softly, standing behind her. "Looks to be the mouth of the temple."

"Temple? Looks like nothing more than a frozen ruin of some kind. How could this be the temple?"

"The temple was never a secret, my dear. Finding it, on the other hand... There lies the challenge."

"I don't understand, Master," she grumbled as she turned to face him in confusion.

"I think I do," Jon said, stepping closer to one of the pillars. "It's buried under all the snow. These pillars must be massive, going twenty feet down into the ground?" he asked Master Kon.

"At least," he told them, his expression unreadable.

"You knew?" Takayo asked. "That's why you wanted me to save my strength?"

Master Kon stepped back from her. He gave Takayo the stern look of someone wishing to impart courage.

"Take in the water around you and move just what is before you first, Takayo. Pace yourself. Just a bit at a time. But please replace what you use; otherwise, the headaches will crush you."

Replace what I use.

She turned and looked at the whiteness before her. What was in front of her was as wide as a field.

Just what is *in front of me?* she thought with more than a bit of curiosity. *How much is in front of me?*

But what was in front of her was vast and daunting. Takayo swallowed, opened up her senses, and took in a large amount of water-air, letting the elements fill her. She closed her eyes and let the elements in the snow and ice speak to her in her elemental mind. She could feel water everywhere. It was in the air. It was in the earth, in the snow and ice. It was floating in the sky above her.

In the beginning, the snow only drifted upward as if it was snowing in reverse, with the snowflakes fluttering back up to the clouds. Then the ground before her thundered, and huge blasts of ice ripped from beneath the surface of the frozen snow-packed earth. Her skull began to feel heavy, reminding Takayo that she was moments away from great pain. She sucked in a lung full of water-air, and the pounding of her mind faded.

Jon jumped backward as a massive slab of ice punched the surface of the hillside just before Takayo, and when she opened her eyes, she saw the long spike of ancient ice moving according to her commands. The slab tore a crater before her, and a hole gaped in the earth under her feet. A waterfall of fresh powder threatened to fill the void, but as she grabbed the elements within the ice, the snow erupted over their heads. It sent significant bits of ice fragments rocketing down around them in a freezing hail storm.

Weakness overcame her, and a blast of winter chill tossed Takayo to her knees.

"Takayo!" Jon yelled, running to her. His tiny hands pulled her close as the familiar pain filled her mind. Takayo closed her eyes as Jon held her in his shivering arms. She let her face settle into the slope of his shoulder and breathed in a mouthful of crisp air. It filled her lungs, sending a chill over her body. After a time, Takayo took in the water elements around her. The water moved into her cells, filling her with hydration. Slowly her thoughts cleared and strength returned to her limbs once again.

"I'm okay, Jon," she told him encouragingly, climbing back to her feet. Next to her, the crater waited like the gaping mouth of some great sea creature swimming up from the ocean's depths to swallow her ship whole. At several points, the snow had slid back into the opening in the earth, closing it off to her.

"As you use your power, Takayo, take the water into you," Master Kon told her again. He was telling her things that she already knew. He was telling her things he had told her a dozen times, yet she couldn't remember them in her excitement. For some reason, she always seemed to forget when it came to reabsorbing the water elements.

She told herself you must replenish what you use, looking down into the void before her.

The water-air entered her quickly enough, and the elemental contact formed almost effortlessly. Yet as she moved wisps of snow from the hole's edge, Takayo wondered if she was determined to do it. Did she have enough skill to dig down so deep? The water within the stone stairs felt as if it called out to Takayo now, almost telling her where she needed to stand. Just then, as she doubted herself, the snowy ground under her feet gave way, and she crashed painfully to the icy edge of whatever was under the earth. The impact was sharp, and pain bit her with thin spikes of agony.

"Ash and embers!" she cursed as she rolled off her bruised ribs. As she slowly tried to roll off the unburied staircase, the frozen stone steps under her dug in with every movement. The ice under her was slick, and her footing slipped, causing Takayo to tumble closer to the edge of the large hole.

"That looked like it hurt," Master Kon said, suddenly beside her.

"Yes... I—"

"Got weak?" he asked her with a smile that said, 'I told you to take the water in.'

"I know, I know, Master."

"Knowing is one thing, but remembering is another," he said.

She spun on her heels and looked down the white steps at her feet. Ice caked the flight of large stairs that sloped into the great hole and sunk into the snow at its base. She sucked in water-air again and moved the snow at the bottom of the stairs. This time it turned into a mist of hydration, and she pushed the water into her body. Even though the water brought her cells racing back to life and held back the pain in her skull, the chill of its wetness shocked Takayo, making her shiver as she replenished her strength.

Once she'd had her fill of hydration, she dug deep into the ice and snow before her with her mind, exploding the ground, shaking and rumbling the earth at her feet. The snow swam upward like a living thing desperately trying to run from a predator. The white powder washed up high over the bank of the massive hole, hissing as it moved over packed snowy hills.

The pain in her brain pinged her again, and Takayo sucked in the elements once more. She took a long, cleansing breath as she looked down upon the surface of a frozen temple courtyard that hadn't seen the light of day in a thousand years. At the base of the long slick staircase were ancient stone benches flanking the square. In the center of the stone circle, she could see signs of carvings and what looked to be a face, stern and intimidating, staring back at her from the snow with angry eyes.

"What is that?" Jon asked innocently from behind her. His words startled her. She had forgotten he was there. Takayo had forgotten about both of them. In her thoughts, it was just her and the snow temple of the Dragon King.

"This is it? This is the house of the gods?" she asked.

"This is it," Master Kon told her.

Takayo moved down the staircase, careful not to slip, which she nearly did on the first step. The closer she got to the odd carving of the face, the stranger she felt. Looking upon it sent chills up and down her back, and not from the cold either.

At the base of the stairs, she stood outside the stone circle of the temple. The nose and eyes of the figure poked from the depths of the snow like a seedling breaking the surface of the soil for the first time. Getting closer, Takayo brushed bits of flaked ice and snow from around the cheeks and worked to unbury the chin.

"It appears to be a carved stone of some kind," she yelled up to Master Kon and Jon, who were still up at the mouth of the hole.

"Cover stones were used to protect someone important from grave robbers in ancient times. This is most likely someone important."

Takayo moved more snow off from around the features of the face. She knew it before she said aloud, "It's *him*, Master. I recognize his face from my vision. This is the resting place of the Dragon King."

"This can't be, Takayo," Master Kon said. "The Dragon Kings died in the God Wars in another world from here. Their bodies were never seen in this world again."

Takayo stood back from the cover stone and looked upon the likeness of the Dragon King with an uneasy feeling. She raised her hand and used the water elements to push off the remaining snowflakes from the top of the cover stone. This revealed an elaborate full-body carving of a man all in armor, complete with a shield and sword in hand. The snow flakes blew away as if the winter winds came down with a gust just for her. She stared at the bare stone and wondered what she should do next.

"What are you waiting for?" Jon asked from above. "Open it."

"How?! It must weigh close to five hundred pounds."

"Use the elements. The rock must be porous after so long under the ice, Takayo," Master Kon told her. Yet she still shot him a doubtful look. "The Dragon King would have wanted his Reflection to be able to open his tomb, Takayo. Just try it."

Takayo took in a reasonable amount of the water around her and closed her eyes, searching for the elements within the stone. Shockingly, the stone answered her call with several water elements ready to move to her will. As if the vast slab floated on the wind, Takayo took hold of the cover stone and slid it out of its resting home. The bottom of the rough, carved stone scraped and scratched across the courtyard circle as Takayo released her elemental grip upon it. The weight roared back to the stone, and thumped to the ground, sending massive cracks rippling through the face and torso of the sculpture of the Dragon King. She wondered what the god might think of her now. She was invading the tomb in such an aggressive way... But this is what he wanted. She was sure of it. He had sent her here for this, right? The Dragon King had sent her here; clearly, she was meant for this.

Takayo leaned closer to the darkness within the tomb. She scooted nearer to the cavern in the temple—dragging her feet inch by hesitant inch—but the closer she drew to the grave, the louder the water inside the tomb spoke to her. Words sang into her thoughts, but she couldn't make them out, as if they were whispers lost on the wind, but words just the same.

"What do you see?" Jon asked.

"Nothing. Master, do you have some light?"

"*I* do!" That was all the excuse that little Jon needed. He ran down the icy steps to her, nearly losing his footing several times. When he reached her, he thrust a small hand-held lantern at her. Its flame almost went out with his sloppy motion, but then it grew brave and brighter on its oil wick. Takayo twisted the tiny brass wheel, and the flame grew brighter.

"Thank you, Jon."

The two kneeled closer to the edge of the tomb. Takayo could hear Jon's excitement in his breath, his heart pounding next to hers. She held up the lantern, and it pushed back the blackness, shooting light into the long shallow tomb before them.

"Where is he?" Jon asked with his usual childlike curiosity.

"Probably was never here, Jon." Takayo leaned in and dug into the blowing dust and snow on the tomb floor. Her fingers searched for many minutes before they found something hard and metallic.

"There," she finally said.

"What?"

"I found something." She grabbed the object, but it was either too heavy or wasn't meant to be lifted out.

"Please help me, Jon. Let's see if we can dig away the dust around it so I can see what it is."

"Okay, yeah." He seemed nervous but didn't want to disappoint her.

Dust and snow danced as Jon and Takayo dug their fingers into the open tomb. Their hands came up with scoop after scoop of dirty snow until they found the golden lid.

"What do you think it is? Treasure?"

"I have no idea," Takayo patiently answered, grabbing the edges of what felt like a box. The Box was remarkably heavy and required both to lift it clear of the tomb. They raised the heavy lid, which resisted their grasp, and Takayo's fingers snapped back into her palms.

"Ouch! Let's try that again. It's really heavy."

"Okay."

Jon leaned in, and they each took an edge. The old crude hinges whined as the lid slowly opened before them.

"I don't get it," Jon said, holding up the lamp for her. "What is it?"

Takayo grabbed what looked like a long dragon neck and head carved into an elaborate sword hilt. She held it up, inspecting it, moving the dragon hilt in her fingers. The mouth of the dragon was wide open and formed the hilt guard. The dragon's neck formed the handle, but there was no blade. She stared at it for a long time, turning it over in her hands, unsure what to do with it. She could feel the elements within the blade, but when Takayo attempted to connect with the elements, nothing happened.

"Looks to be a sword handle of some kind," she said. "But where is the blade?"

"It could have been destroyed in battle. Or the ages might have destroyed it," Kon told her.

"So what can I do with this?"

"It's a god weapon. And even though it has no blade, it may still be powerful... Do you feel anything when you hold it?"

"I don't know... maybe... Hugh!" she grunted.

Ash and embers.

"I came all this way for *this*?!" Takayo yelled up to Master Kon.

"The gods wanted you to have it for a reason, child. By all rights, it is yours. You are their Reflection."

"By all rights? I don't want this! What am I to do with an empty sword hilt? This does not help me!" She threw the dragon hilt to her feet and stomped off, yet she was somewhat aware of Jon picking it up and putting it into his oversized pocket.

"Let's go!" she yelled in irritation to Jon behind her as she stormed clumsily back up the icy stairs.

4

M aster Kon's bedroom door was unlocked and unlatched. Inside, the darkness for Kanon was complete, his outstretched fingers the only eyes he possessed. The room smelled of honey, jasmine incense, and the green teas that Master Kon was fond of. Kanon reminisced about his old master while stepping closer to his writing table in the center of the room. On the table, it felt primarily free of paper and quills, yet Kanon's hands moved over the items carefully just the same.

This was the first day since Kanon had removed his bandages, and things were not going as well as he had hoped.

"Mouse-mat," he spoke out, "look for any sign that speaks to you as odd or strange."

"Yes, my Lord." The boy was hesitant in the room doorway as if entering might constitute some grave injustice to Master Kon.

Kanon moved slowly over the cold stones—his bare feet rubbing over tiny bits of sand—and his toes found small dust particles. His fingers clumsily stumbled over papers and books that Kanon recalled were the histories of Hisan. Across from the desk sat Master Kon's Hisan-Butsudan, or meditation alter. It featured a small red cabinet with locked doors, and Kanon knew what would be in the cupboard. What was always in the cabinet? The Hachiman Scroll is the first words written about the god of war.

"Mouse-mat," Kanon said, moving over to it slowly. He raised his hands before him as he inched his way closer to it.

"The cabinet... Open the cabinet for me," Kanon said, fumbling a hand under Master Kon's desk and finding the hidden key he knew was there. He snatched it up and produced it for Mouse-mat.

"Open it and tell me what you see. Is it the Hachiman Scroll?"

Mouse-mat was quiet as he picked up the scroll and unrolled it.

"There is a scroll, my Lord, but it is not the Hachiman Scroll. It's—"

"What, boy? Tell me!"

"It appears that Master Kon has left you a note," Mouse-mat told him simply.

"What does it say? Read it to me."

"Yes, Sir. '*Kanon*'—"

"Wait! Close the door first," Kanon said, sliding into a seat at the desk. It creaked at his weight. "We can't have any ears listening in on this."

The door slid closed, protesting as Mouse-mat pulled the lattice shut.

"Now read, Mouse-mat."

Kanon, when I followed you to this place so long ago, I did it to protect you. But there is no protection. It is all an illusion. However, I taught you the best way I could and gave you my knowledge in the way of the warrior. I am proud to see you grow to the man that you are.

I have to leave you in this place, and it is a dangerous place. Someone else is in need of me—someone who needs my help more than you—and I must go to them now. There is no time to find you and say goodbye, but one day we will see one another again, I promise you that.

Those things that you wanted to know about—the things I stopped you from finding—they will lead you to answers, but perhaps answers you're not ready to know. If you want them, remember these words my boy: See through the village and see nothing.

Mouse-mat fell silent, and Kanon heard him set the scroll down. Kanon had thought he knew what he would find in the room. He never expected to see his old sword master but never thought he would find such a message.

'*See nothing,*' he thought. *What does that mean?*

What answers could Kanon get from that? Then Kanon remembered Master Kon's teachings and his training in deep meditation. The purpose of meditation is nothingness. To clear the mess of daily life from your mind and to be at peace with the void.

Master Kon's meditation lessons were simple: start with a quiet village—a village complete with flowering cherry blossoms and swimming koi in a rippling brook. You start with the whole town and then take away one thing daily. You take elements away until you have nothing left, he recalled.

"See through the village..." Kanon said softly.

"What, my Lord?" Mouse-mat turned to face him.

"Oh, nothing. I was just talking to myself."

Did Master Kon want Kanon to meditate? And did he expect him to meditate here or somewhere else? Could he find what Master Kon wanted him to know by clearing his mind? With that thought, another one of his lessons came to him again.

"Zen is nothing, and when you rid yourself of the clutter that your mind does not need, the answers you seek will find you. Clear your mind. *Become* Zen and find the truth."

Kanon gently slid off the chair at the table and moved down onto his knees. He was relatively sure that he was close to Master Kon's altar. He found Master Kon's sa-fu cushion and kneeled on it, sitting on his feet in Zazen meditation. Kanon had never really liked meditation before, and he didn't understand why Master Kon would spend hours of his day in deep meditation either in his room or his dojo.

Many of the Bushi Gos that Master Kon trained over the years complained that many hours of their training required Zazen meditation. Once when Kanon asked Master Kon about it, he told him that the eyes reveal the spirit and the soul and that they will give you away every time. If you are angry or excited, you cannot do anything as well as when you are calm. Zazen meditation relaxes one's mind, spirit, and body.

"My Lord?" Mouse-mat asked, noticing what Kanon was doing.

"Leave me be, Mouse-mat. I think I will stay here."

"As you wish. Ring for me if you have need, Master."

"Very good."

Kanon waited for the sound of the lattice door sliding shut, confirming that he was utterly alone.

"Okay, see through the village," he told himself.

Kanon fell into meditation the same way he always had, and Over the next half hour, Kanon repeated the process several times, and with each exhale, he felt his body relax a little bit more. After he thought that his body had reached the desired state of relaxation, Kanon pictured the village in his mind, just as Master Kon had told him to do.

Kanon's record for this village exercise was not excellent. In fact, he could only get rid of a few buildings and one of the cherry trees in the past. Yet he pictured it now, all the same. The village painted itself on the canvas of his mind. Its soft pastels of reds and pinks worked through the tiny blossoms of the cherry trees and into the coming sunrise over the mountains behind the village.

So far, the thought of the village gave him some sense of peace.

Why couldn't this be Zen? He liked it here. He wanted to be here. The village looked like pictures of the Soulchemy towns in the Uenhal Mountain range in the north. Beauty that he would never see now…

He watched the village in his thoughts and heard the rippling water of a stream move under an arched wooden bridge. Birds took to the air. He saw dozens of cherry blossom petals dance in a soft, cooling breeze that moved over several small wooden homes. He saw the massive mountain that sat silently looming, its vast body in the background of his village. Its sloping peak was white with winter snow.

After an hour, the world around him seemed oddly quiet. He had only meant to take away a few birds, but when he looked at the village now, not only were the birds gone, but so was the rippling water. Where a moment ago, an ankle-deep stream of spring water cut a path down the countryside, now only grass stood its place. Even the arched bridge hunched over the wet brook was no more than a lost memory.

Kanon fought to keep his thoughts calm as he felt himself waver slightly. A faint glow of the bridge came back to his thoughts for only an instant. He quickly refocused his mind and cut out all the distractions of his immediate surroundings. He watched as, once again, the bridge faded away.

Suddenly another flash of light exploded in his mind. It blinded him with sights. The view of his bedroom's balcony came to life, illuminated in grays and whites before him. Tall towers of substantial black stones and thick mortar stood hulking, looming overhead like monstrous structures looking back at him. The markets below the balcony looked colorless. The view was as if it was from the very base of the ground as if a pebble of stone was the eye through which Kanon now saw. The blue-less sky above pushed white clouds out of his frame of sight.

It wasn't like seeing through his own eyes, not really. But it was something else. At once, the vision moved away from the city's sights and ran into darkness. The city's light fled as the rat whose eyes Kanon now saw through ran into the night of a nearby hole. The evening was all-consuming, pushing blindness back to Kanon. His heart shot beats under his chest as he clawed and struggled to his feet. Kanon stumbled blindly, toppling over the tableside chair, and Kanon and the chair went sprawling onto the hard, cold floor.

"What?!" Kanon struggled upright, scrabbling for a piece of the table next to him. "Ash and embers! For the love of the gods! What do you want from me?" he roared, kicking the chair careening off the wall of Master Kon's room. Again he stumbled in the darkness, but he caught himself.

I don't understand. I saw. *How is that possible*? Kanon thought, cursing to himself.

He did see but then did not see. There was no view of the markets from Master Kon's rooms, he remembered. The vision must have been from his chambers.

See past the village. The words snapped into his thoughts again.

What is happening to me?

Kanon sat defeated on his knees in the center of Master Kon's room, the chair on its side well out of Kanon's grasp. He tipped his head back and focused.

"Calm. When you are upset, you will accomplish nothing," Kanon murmured. "Only clear-headed thoughts will find the answers."

Kanon struggled to calm himself. He was young and hot-headed. Those words Master Kon had used to describe Kanon once, and they stuck with him. At the time, the words had cut deep, but they had an impact upon the young prince now. They focused his mind, and now he let those words center him again.

"Calm yourself and then think. There is a definite connection. There is a power in Zazen," he reminded himself. Those words were spoken once by Kon too. "Zen is a form of the ascension of the mind. It will bring you close to the gods. When you find true Zen, you open the door to your mind."

But he hadn't reached Zen, not all the way. Yet something had occurred while Kanon was briefly in Zazen. He felt a power, a presence that he had not felt before, as if Kanon wasn't alone in the secrecy of his mind. Had he let something in? Let some*one* in?

He did *see*; he reminded himself. Was it a vision, or did his eyes pick something up? Kanon wondered. He wasn't any closer to understanding this strange sight, but one thing seemed clear. He needed to meditate again if he wanted his answers.

A final flash blasted against Kanon's mind, sending him slipping back to the cold floor. The back of his skull smacked the wide stones. Through blurry inner vision, Kanon saw the Empress surrounded by darkness. She stood before the reflection well that she kept in her room. Kanon had seen it several times, but this was different. He had never seen it like this before. The Empress withdrew a long, bladed knife from next to the well, and she pushed several inches of its thin point into her arm's dry, loose flesh. The weathered skin around the slits of her eyes grew even more drawn with age as the blade entered her flesh. For an instant, she looked far more aged than Kanon had ever known her to be. A stream of black blood slipped out the open slice in her flesh and bled into the black water of the well before her. Kanon lay still on the ground as he watched her stick her hand into the bloody water and stir the blood and the water together.

"My blood to your blood," he heard her say as she stooped over the well. "My life to your life. Death to death, hear me now—"

The vision wavered in his mind blurred even deeper. Suddenly it was gone, and there was only blackness.

"No!" Kanon desperately climbed to his feet and dangerously ran for Master Kon's lattice door. Finding it, he threw it to the side, nearly sending it off its wooden track. He stumbled down the hall in darkness. He ran around a corner and nearly collided with the small end table there, yet it did not stop Kanon from running as fast as he could toward where he knew his mother's room. The darkness was complete as he ran, and corners flew by him quickly and dangerously, each step bringing him closer and closer until he found her private chamber.

Through the doorway came the soft trilling sounds of a songbird mingled with the murmurs of a conversation. The thick walls muffled the voices, yet as Kanon crept closer, the voices moved into his audible range. He pressed an ear to the cold surface of her chamber door and listened as best he could.

The Empress talked with someone Kanon had never before heard in his life. The stranger's voice sounded like a cross between a bear and an ox. The low guttural sounds of the person's voice unnerved him as Kanon strained to hear.

"Before time was time, I ruled this land and took the dead into my care. Do you remember that, woman?" the voice snapped in anger.

"I remember."

"When you came before me, you were nothing but a scared little girl who didn't want to lose her soul. You climbed the steps of my throne, humble and penitent. Secure in the knowledge of what you were. You knew your life would be short, lessened by what you were. I gave you what you needed and longevity, a power over the world."

"Yes. You did."

"That was a millennia ago, and you still live... And what of me? What of our deal? Still, I sit—half in this world and half in yours—trapped inside that small weak frame that you call a body, too weak to do anything. Give me what I need, woman! Or I will take your soul as payment once and for all."

"You already took the life of the last Soulchemist, and it was not enough to bring you..." the Empress told the voice calmly.

"Yes... And I will have the life of the next as well. The previous Soulchemist was far too old. His soul had been lessened too many times, but this boy... His soul is whole. There is much to work with."

"We are close," the Empress said.

"Close? You don't have the boy yet? You told me that you would!" The dark voice roared, and the door under Kanon's ear thumped.

"And so we shall. We have his location."

"Then send your soldiers and get me my Soulchemist. Now! Finish what you started so long ago."

5

Nothing hurts as bad as being disappointed.

These words sounded in Takayo's mind as she stomped from the Temple of the Dragon King. She didn't look at Jon or Master Kon as she moved past them on the icy stone staircase of the temple.

"Takayo, I think the gods meant for you to—"

"No, Master Kon. No. Let us just find your friend. Let's do something right. I came to the temple and found what the Dragon King meant for me to find. Now let us be off and done with it. Okay?"

"As you wish, Takayo."

For the next several hours, it wasn't Master Kon that led them out and away from the mountain but Takayo. However, it would be more accurate to say that her anger led them. She stomped and furiously pushed on through the deep snow. Not one word passed her lips for a good part of the day, but when they returned to the location where Mika's blood had been the previous day, her anger had softened a bit. She moved back as Master Kon looked for clues, hoping for a sign telling them where to go. Finding none, Master Kon moved out to where they had first encountered the marks in the trees.

"We're getting closer. Right, Takayo?" Jon asked as they walked together behind Master Kon.

"I think so. I remember this being one of the last areas where we spotted the marks on the way up to the temple," she told him.

"I'm sorry you didn't find what you were looking for at the temple, Takayo," he said apologetically.

"It's okay... I just wanted some answers."

Jon pulled the sword hilt from his coat, unwrapped it, and held it up for her. "You still might find some answers in this," he said. She looked at it long before taking the dragon hilt in her hands. She smiled for the first time since she had laid eyes upon the ancient hilt.

"It *is* rather beautiful," Takayo told him, rolling the hilt in her fingers and admiring the workmanship. "Artfully crafted for a god."

"It must have once been part of a sword," Jon said somberly.

She held the hilt up to the light. "No sign of a blade of any kind. There's a clear tunnel from the pummel to the hilt. I would think we would see some hint of a blade, even after this long, if it had been broken off. But there does seem to be some sort of clear crystal in the deep throat of the dragon."

"I wonder what the writing is on the side there," Jon asked, pointing to the side of the hilt.

"Mika will be able to tell us. He will be able to tell you all that you need to know, Takayo," Master Kon said without looking back at them.

"Really?"

"Master Mika is our historian of the gods and the God Wars. He will know what that is. So you see, you may still have the answers you seek."

Takayo thought about that momentarily and stared down at the dragon hilt in her hands. There was something about it when she held the hilt... There was something different in how she felt when she touched it. Something suddenly changed, mutated inside her. She became oddly aware of the elements around her more than ever. They felt clearer and more powerful, moving closer to Takayo, ready for her communication. She dropped the hilt into a side pocket of her coat, and instantly the connection lessoned.

Well, that is something, she thought, mystified.

Just as Takayo was about to reach into her pocket and test the hilt again, Master Kon took off in a flat-out run.

"Master... what is it?" she called after him with trepidation.

"A blood trail was frozen into the ice."

Takayo and Jon ran as fast as they could through the thick powder. Her feet struggled to keep up with the determined, sure footing of Master Kon. With every step, Kon drew farther and farther from

Takayo. Though she worked to keep pace with him, she could not. After several frustrated turns and sprints by Master Kon, Takayo was sufficiently frustrated enough to thrust a hand into her pocket and take hold of the hilt. Without even having to make the connection with the water elements around her, Takayo's steps lightened as her body shot forward like a bird in flight. Her toes grazed the white snow, and in an instant, the long space between Master Kon and Takayo was only a few feet. Master Kon's back thundered closer and closer to her faster than she thought it might. She called back the elements, but the momentum was too fast to stop, and she raced past the rushing steps of Master Kon, who was unaware of her snowy flight. Her furs lashed out at his face as her body blurred past him, causing the sword master to stumble and Takayo to crash into the soft snow before him.

"What in the name of the gods?" Master Kon said, touching the trickle of blood on his cheek from where the furs had whipped him. He looked down at Takayo, a mess of fur and clumps of snow. She struggled to her feet as Master Kon reached for her.

"What was that, Takayo?"

"I don't really know," she said, dusting herself off. "I sort of... flew I guess."

"What do you mean you 'flew'?" he asked as Jon finally reached them, entirely out of breath.

"The sword hilt seems to boost my connection with the elements. Like when I used the elements to slow myself when I fell. I—"

"You used them to push you forward?" Master Kon said.

"Well, yes. I mean, you were getting so far away. And I just couldn't catch up. I don't know what I meant to do when I reached for the hilt. It just sort of... happened."

"The elements felt your need, Takayo."

"But I didn't even know. I mean, I didn't even ask them to..."

"The elements are inside you as well, Takayo. It may get to a point where you won't need to ask them or even think. They may just react for you," Master Kon said.

"You flew, Takayo!" Jon said.

"*Pushed* is what it felt like," she said. "As if the gods had scooped me up and threw me at Master Kon."

"You might get to a point where you could take flight if the air is wet enough. During a snowstorm, or at sea perhaps," Master Kon told her, smiling at her feet.

"Something else too, Master. I felt another element. I was aware of the wind at my back and the water."

"That, too, makes some sense to me. If the gods intend for you to fly using the water-air, they would want you to be able to use the wind or the air pressure as well. But for now, put the hilt away until we find Mika. I'm glad you found what you were looking for, Takayo."

Master Kon turned and moved deeper into the snow. He ran, taking several turns, and then suddenly stopped at the mouth of a trailhead flanked by two hulking cliffs of white ice.

"What is it?" Jon asked, mystified.

"The doorway is open."

"Doorway?" Takayo asked. It suddenly occurred to her that this had been a locked passageway to a village. Now, the door was no longer locked, and she knew why.

"Come on, let's move," Master Kon said without looking back at them.

The doorway is open. I did this. My actions did this. Whatever we find on the other side of this door is all my doing.

The smoldering wisps of smoke moved overhead like a blackened snake slithering into the sky, its thin tail pointing down to the carnage below.

"Do you see that?" Master Kon asked, looking up into the sky.

"A campfire?" Jon asked.

"That is no campfire. It carries the scent of death with it."

Takayo moved past Jon and Master Kon down a thin snaking trail. Pale mists rose before her from the white earth as they threaded through the scattering of snowcapped trees, icy stones, and crunching ground down toward the unwelcoming fires strewn about before them like a warning telling them to keep away. There were more dying fires than she had ever seen or could count, hundreds of fires whose smoke painted the sky black.

They descended the ridge without a word, disturbed by the horrid scent of death gagging the air. The quiet was only broken by the distant crackling of the closest dying fire. Before long, it was made clear to all what they were seeing. The scent of death and the black smoke told the story of the massacre and the destruction of life.

"What is this place?" Takayo asked.

"A village of simple people. The home of the Uenhal family clan," Master Kon said.

"The Soulchemist?" Takayo asked. Her eyes shot to one of the burning piles of bodies. "I did this. I gave them this."

"No, Takayo. This was Shihan's doing. Not yours. I blame her as you should."

But Takayo did blame Shihan for this; she only blamed herself.

At the bottom of the slope, they came upon a small trickle of a stream flowing down from the mountain's foothills to join the Soulchemy village's water source. The water cut across their path and snaked to the side as they came to the mouth of the town, shielded by massive trees. Master Kon led them across a creaky old bridge that moaned painfully as the three walked over the village stream.

Takayo stopped at the sight before her: eight men about fighting age lay dead just inside the village entrance. Some women and boys were thrown together in piles, clad in fur and boiled leather. A turned-over helm had stepped into the caked earth. None were armed with spears or axes—not one had so much as a smithing hammer—but all were executed. Bushi arrows littered the ground and the wooden houses on the outskirts of the courtyard.

With some urging from Master Kon, Takayo moved past burning, smoldering piles of the dead villagers.

"I don't understand," Jon said, bewildered. "The Shadou-wāgu were supposed to protect them. Protect the Soulchemist. Right, Master?"

"*We* were supposed to protect him. I don't know about the Shadou-wāgu."

Takayo wanted to ask who the Shadou-wāgu were and why those people did not do something to help these poor villagers. She wanted to ask, but she just didn't have the strength as she moved closer and closer to the piles of burnt flesh. She stopped by the village water house, a small stone-covered shelter in the courtyard's center. Horrible imagery filled Takayo's vision, and her mind was filled with one thought: *I did this*.

Ash fell from the snowy sky. She watched embers and flakes drift through the air. Leisurely, almost carelessly. The puffs of burnt ash fell like bits of rose blossoms blowing in the breeze. They floated in the corners of her hair and curled in tiny whirlwinds over her shoulders as they danced around her. Takayo dropped to her knees, and tears ran from her burning eyes.

So many dead. So many innocent lives. Just... gone.

The young face of a child dressed in simple clothes looked back at her beneath the charred blackness of one of the fire pits. The dead eyes sent chills surging throughout her, and for a very long, tense moment, Takayo couldn't take the sight of it all. She forced her eyes shut and felt the pressure of several tears push past her lids and fall clear of her face.

Master Kon reached down and gently took her by the shoulder, pulling her close for a comforting embrace. She let him do it. She let her face fall flat into the caverns of his chest, and then she cried sobs into the snowy fur of his wolf pelts.

"The Bushi?" She cried the question.

"Yes."

"So they have him then?" she asked, pulling back from Master Kon and looking up at him.

"No... they do not."

"What?"

"If they had found the Soulchemist, they would have taken the boy. They wouldn't have done this. They killed these people because Roa is *not* here. And neither is Mika."

"Well..." she started and stood up, wiping her face, "then what do we do?"

"If Mika was in trouble, he would have led Roa away from the village and headed toward the nearest Shinto-Kamie ship."

"So where is that?"

"Shi," Jon spoke up suddenly. "They must have headed to Shi."

Takayo rubbed at her eyes with the back of her gloved hands, pushing her pain deep down. She gave her friends a look of focus. It was all she could muster at that moment.

"Are you alright, Takayo?"

"No, none of this is alright," she confessed. But I will be."

"We need to move. I know this was hard to see, but I need both of you to gather your strength if we are to make it to the mountain's base by sunset."

"Okay."

The wind blew wet and heavy as they crossed the valley and moved south down the mountain by the river. Jon kept close to Takayo, but she hadn't felt like talking, so the distance between the two felt uncomfortable. Her steps grew with her anticipation, and just as Master Kon had turned his pace to nearly a run, so had Takayo, leaping over and around corners and lobbing herself between trees.

Once more, she breathed in the snowy air around her, taking one of the corners with much risk. She leaped over a mound of powder, and as she did, she moved the water close to her. She nearly laughed at the feeling of her feet skimming over the rocks, landing in front of Master Kon. Takayo shot her teacher a youthful look and jumped again. He was powerless to pull her back. There was a part of Takayo that felt that this was the point. This was the reason that he pushed them so hard to the mountain. He wanted her to do this. After all, this was why they were there—to uncover the artifact and to see what Takayo could do with it. Though a part of her felt that the Dragon Hilt was cheating, touching it and getting her elemental boost was skipping a step in her progression.

Her limbs flapped like a bird riding a breeze high in the sky. Tiny snow-covered branches slapped her face and shoulders as she rose high over yearling trees. Jon's voice was a distant memory below her as she flew. The water held her for several heartbeats. Then at the peak of her ascent, the wind came back at her hair, ripping the long locks from her face as she plummeted back down to earth. The ground came fast, faster than she had hoped it would. She took the water in the snow at the last possible moment and pushed on it with everything she had. The snow under her compacted instantaneously, and her body slowed just enough to keep her from any real damage, yet the impact was painful.

Takayo's face slammed and slid over ice and rock. The trees near her tumbled around and around before finally halting behind her. Her eye stung, and she saw not a thing. But she could hear the running steps of her companions. One set of steps, particularly those of Master Kon, soon stopped before her.

"Let me guess," he spoke out of the blackened cold to her. "You forgot to take in the water again?"

"Huh... I didn't think I needed to when I have the hilt," she said, climbing to her feet.

"And where is the hilt, Takayo?" Master Kon said, brushing snow off of her.

"Well, um... in my pocket," she said, pushing her fingers into the deep pocket of her furs.

"And were you holding the hilt during that great high-flying feat just now?" he asked.

"Well, I…"

"If you're not going to let god work through you, then you need to follow the rules," Master Kon said, moving past her. "And what are the rules, young student?"

"Take in the water," she droned and continued to follow him down the mountain. She caught a smile from Jon, who snickered behind her.

6

This was something Takayo knew about herself: Her mind made miscalculations sometimes, and her body reacted without the process of her mind. Her body was a traitor to levelheaded thinking.

She lowered her hand into her coat and felt the hilt. Her fingers moved in the darkness against the cold length of it hidden in her pocket. She took her icy hand and rubbed it on the metal. She heard the echo of a voice in her mind as she moved in silence past the edge of the thick trees. Suddenly, the last hint of the sun's glow faded over the rippling waves of the black water.

Her eyes gazed over the star-sprinkled night above the long, rich brushstrokes of color fading into the horizon.

"We're out of the village," she said, walking up to Master Kon.

"Yes, but soon there will not be enough light to see a foot in front of us. We must move quickly now."

The three of them hurried down a snaking trail that led to the waterline at the base of the mountain, inked by the coming night. By the time the cold waves of the black water touched her feet, Takayo could scarcely see a hint of the fading fingers of light from the sinking sun. She found Master Kon was in a somewhat melancholy mood. He was on one knee, seemingly without care that the water line had soaked his pants or that his toes had been consumed by sodden sand.

"What is it?" she asked, kneeling to him.

"Blood. Not as bad as it was up in the mountains. It was left here on purpose. That I'm sure of now."

"How can you be so certain, Master?" Jon asked, stepping forward.

"He would have healed long before this. Mika is keeping his wound fresh. I would stake my life on it. He would know that someone would be looking for him if something like this happened—and he was truly in trouble. The blood is faint, and most of it has washed away by the water, but he must be no more than a day ahead of us."

"How can you know that?" Jon asked, curiosity warring with respect in his voice.

"The tides, my boy. The tide is now coming in. It will consume this whole beach in the next two hours. The blood was put here after the last tide, after yesterday's tide. Otherwise, it would have already been washed clean. Understand?"

"Yes, Master."

The three of them moved on for the next few minutes, walking several feet from one another. They searched the area in what Master Kon called a 'marching line.' They formed a row, walking about ten feet from one another, and looked for any sign of Mika's presence that they could see in the moonlight.

For several minutes, Takayo was unaware of the others. She was oblivious to Kon and Jon moving faster than her or that they had spotted something. It was at that moment that she sensed something. Her fingers were back on the hilt again. The mind she felt was near. So near it seemed inside her head now. It wasn't talking to her, exactly. Yet she heard it enough as if she was spying on a conversation. Some underhanded purpose consumed the strange mind. All a very good reason to draw her attention away from the task at hand. It wasn't the voice of the Dragon God—she seemed sure of that. However, the voice seemed to be one of familiarity—one that she didn't know but then did.

It was a guilty mind—a spiteful one.

Takayo could not ignore it or simply push it from her thoughts. The voice grew louder as she stepped away from their marching line and moved around the cove.

I'll follow it, she thought. *I'll see where it is.*

The sense that moved her now was a foreign one, yet at the same time, it tingled in her memory. She looked into the shadows of her mind. The sense was there, just beyond the shadows—hiding from her now—yet it drew her down her path.

Takayo was astonished momentarily when a rough hand pulled her back from her quest. It happened all so fast. She didn't mean to do it. She had been startled. She was already holding the hilt, and the elements within her were already activated. She spun around, swinging the hilt in defense out of muscle memory, when suddenly a blast of water erupted from the dragon hilt and instantly froze into a jagged, razor-sharp blade the length of her arm. It sliced the air, nearly taking Master Kon's head off. He jumped back into a defensive stance as a thin line opened on his cheek. An instant later, the blade was gone, melted, and raining down on Takayo's feet in huge drops of water.

"Master! Are you alright?" she said fearfully, dropping the hilt.

"What...? I..." He shot two fingers to his face and felt the trickle of blood.

"I'm so sorry. I don't know what happened," Takayo said mournfully, staring at the hilt on the ground. Master Kon smiled and relaxed his stance.

"I do, Takayo. This is certainly a god weapon. A true blade meant for you. You channeled the elements into the hilt."

"I... what?"

"Don't you get it yet, girl?" Master Kon said, snatching the hilt from the ground with some annoyance. "This is the sword of the Ice Dragon. A gift from the gods! Amazing. Absolutely amazing."

"I don't know how I did it," she had to admit to him. Kon looked at her for a very long time before he spoke again.

"I think I do. You told me what you did on *The Black Dog*, and it's what just happened now. You got scared. Your emotion and fear brought your power out of you. Fear is good. It keeps us alive and lets us protect ourselves and those around us. We will work on this." His lips pulled tight across his face as he beamed down at Takayo holding the Dragon Hilt out for her to take.

"What were you doing anyway, Takayo?" Jon asked after a moment of silence. "You sure weren't searching for signs of Master Mika."

"I heard a voice. Truth be told, I've been hearing a voice for the last several hours."

"What?!" Master Kon exclaimed and rushed over to her side once more. "Why didn't you say something?"

"I was going to, I just—"

"Was it the god?" he needed to know.

"I don't think so. I mean, it didn't feel like the god. Like any god. It was... angry."

"Angry?" Master Kon repeated her word.

"Well, maybe more like the voice didn't like me. Like an angry sibling trying to get me into trouble."

"I don't like this... The voice had a hold on you, Takayo," Master Kon said in a tone tinged with worry. "Now, what did it say?"

"It wasn't really *what* it said, but more about how I felt. The words weren't clear."

"Okay, so how did you feel?"

"Disliked. Almost hated. Yet I couldn't take myself away from what it wanted me to do."

"What did it want you to do?" Jon asked hesitantly.

"Well, I don't really know. But I had an overwhelming desire to leave the group."

"I would say you were doing just that. We found you some thirty yards away from our line."

Master Kon stepped forward and seized Takayo's hand that still held the hilt, suddenly bringing it up into the moonlight.

"Do you hear it now? When you touch the hilt?"

Her gaze fell onto the ancient hilt for a moment and then to Master Kon, who looked concerned.

"Yes, Master."

He pulled a length of silk from his pocket and offered it to her.

"Wrap it in this and put the hilt in your satchel. Keep from touching it until we can have Mika look at it. Some evil spirit or god is part of that weapon. I don't know if it is part of the power or not, but we must not take the chance, Takayo."

Jon and Master Kon watched silently as Takayo carefully wrapped the length of silk around the ancient hilt. She tied it tightly before tucking it into the satchel at her hip.

"Keep it as far away from your skin as you can," Master Kon added before turning from her. Without speaking again, the three formed their line and continued their search for the others.

As Takayo moved in the darkness, no voice came to her. No voice beckoned her, but there was a draw to touch the hilt again. There was a desire to feel its power on her cold flesh, to move her fingers over the artistry of its masterful, godly design. Yet Takayo was strong and did not touch it.

After moving in the darkness over sloping beaches, they came to what looked in the moonlight to be long blades of grass. However, they weren't long blades of grass blowing in the night wind at all.

"What is it?" Jon called over to Kon as the master moved into the field and seized one of the blades into his hand.

"Arrows."

He held out the wooden shaft under a ray of moonlight for the others to see. Takayo looked at the long feathered section held out to her and into the field of arrows that seemed to grow out of the beach before them.

"What happened?" Jon asked innocently.

"Bushi attack," Takayo said before Master Kon could speak.

"Spread out. Look for Mika," he ordered.

Takayo moved slowly around the long shafts of arrows for many minutes before she found it. Nearly stumbling on the mound, she came upon the lifeless body of what looked to be a warrior woman. She had fallen to a large grouping of arrow shafts in her upper back.

"Master!" Takayo called out. She heard Master Kon's sword leave the scabbard and the sound of its edge sheering through the wooden shafts of arrows near her.

"What... what is it, Takayo?" Master Kon called out.

"A dead woman."

Master Kon's long stride closed the gap quickly, and he was at her side. He sheathed his blade and kneeled to the body. The woman had hair as blue as Takayo had ever seen. Kon moved the fallen fighter over, gently snapping the arrows in her back so as not to unintentionally push the arrows deeper into the body. He lifted her eyelids with a gentle touch as he spoke strange words.

"Shadou-wāgu."

"What?" Takayo asked, confused.

"Shadou-wāgu are the warrior clan that has vowed to protect the Soulchemist for hundreds of years. This woman was one of those warriors. She—"

"She...d...did just that, old friend." The voice weakly bled out of the darkness. But the sound of those words sent Master Kon reeling around.

"Mika!" he called out. "Is that you?"

However, for a moment, the words did not come again. The wind howled, yet Takayo was sure she could hear a moaning hidden within the gust of wind.

"Master Kon, I think it came from that direction," she said, pointing over to her left side, away from the waterline.

"Mika, you old fool! Where are you?" Master Kon called out in a friendly voice, trying to sound lighthearted. Yet no voice came back to him.

"Quickly, you two. Spread out. He must be hurt. Takayo, take the left bank. Jon, go down by the water's edge, and I'll go up the middle."

It didn't take Takayo long to see it. The bloody arrow, stained with a dark red smear that traveled half the length of the shaft, and the dragging trail were clear to her.

"Master!" she called out. "I've got something...blood."

Master Kon flew up the snowcapped beach slope, nearly knocking Takayo to the ground.

"Mika! Mika!" he yelled as he flew to his wounded friend. Takayo wasn't sure how Master Kon could see the thin trail of blood in the moonlight, but in only a few hurtling steps, Kon was at his friend's side.

"Mika, open your eyes, my friend." Kon shook Mika's weakened shoulder, careful not to touch the long arrow protruding from the man's torso.

"Augghh—"

"Are you okay? Open your eyes, Mika."

"Do I look okay?"

Takayo and Jon soon descended the hill, and the sight was horrible. The long arrow shaft stuck in the older man's side had stained the snow red and looked to have weakened Mika to death.

"You're okay, old man. We just need to get that arrow out of you," Kon said.

"I... I didn't have the strength."

"Mika, where is the Soulchemist?"

"Gone. The Bushi have him," Mika said, slumping back down. "I'm far too weak, Kon. You need to do it. Please. Pull it out."

"Do you have enough strength to heal? You look weak, old friend."

"Awgh! I've been saving up but knew I couldn't pull it out. If you can... I can heal."

"Hang on."

Master Kon took hold of the arrow as close to Mika's ribs as possible. At first, his fingers slipped on the slick blood, but then the arrow wrenched free, and Mika clapped a hand over the wound. Blood spilled out around and between his fingers for a moment, and then—to

Takayo's shock—the spurts slowed to a trickle and then stopped altogether.

"How...?" Takayo mumbled in awe. She didn't mean to say it out loud, but the words just fell from her mouth.

"It's my Reflection, little one," Mika said, looking up at her with his weakened face. "I can heal very quickly."

"Yes, I know... Master Kon said as much, but..."

"But seeing is different than hearing about it, I know," Master Kon said. Kon shot out a hand to Mika and helped the old man to his feet. "It's so very good to see you again, old friend."

"I never thought I would lay eyes upon the likes of you again, Kon, after what you did. But I understand what brought you there and kept you in the palace, even if others do not."

"Thank you for that," Kon told him humbly.

"Excuse me, Sir," Takayo interrupted them. "But what are we going to do? We need to help the Soulchemist."

"Master Mika," Kon said, "this is Takayo Jin, Dragon King Reflection."

"Dragon King Reflection?" Mika looked at her for some time. His eyes moved over her, studying her, and then he spoke as if he had just decided something.

"The Waterbringer. You're the one that the temple spoke of."

"We just came from the temple, Mika," Kon told him. "The Dragon King sent her there."

"Really?"

"We don't have time for this!" she yelled at them impatiently. "We need to go after the boy."

"Calm yourself, Waterbringer. It is my duty to go after him, and I will. But he has a whole day's travel on us, and I am weak. So we—"

"Then *I* will," she interrupted stubbornly.

"And what are you going to do, Takayo?" Master Kon scolded her. "Storm the palace gates and kill every Bushi you encounter?"

"If I must," she told them with steel. "With the hilt, I can—"

"You can get yourself killed, Takayo! That hilt is as unpredictable as you are. You've come a long way, but this is not what the gods have planned for you."

"How do *you* know what they have planned?"

"Okay, wait. Can we back up a bit?" Mika said. "Did the gods gift you something?"

"A sword hilt," Jon spoke softly behind everyone. Mika turned, and Jon gave him an innocent, childlike grin as an introduction.

"I knew it. The writing on the temple pillars spoke of the Waterbringer and the Dragon King's resting place. If it was the sword wielded by the gods, it may hold great power for you."

"Yes, great power and something else," Master Kon said. "She is hearing voices now."

"Of course, you are, child. You are now connected to anyone who has wielded it before you. Some good and some bad."

"What do you mean?" Master Kon asked, shocked.

"It is a god weapon, but it wasn't always only gods that used it. The Waterbringer that came before you—"

"The one that broke the world!" Takayo said. "I saw it in my vision."

"Vision..." Mika said. "So the gods have actively spoken to you? That is very rare indeed."

"I don't like the voice. She is full of rage and anger."

"Of course she is... She was crazy, and devastated Tranquist at the height of her anger, so that is the voice imprinted upon the hilt."

"Can it hurt me?"

"Only if you let it, child."

"What power..." Mika wondered at her. "How much of the Dragon King gods are in you, Takayo? The first Waterbringer processed power from all the brothers. Her power was massive enough to destroy land and sink cities."

"I only have one of the brother's powers—"

"She is impressive, Mika. Let's leave it at that."

Mika and Kon looked at one another for some time, and it seemed to Takayo as if they were having a wordless conversation. After a sigh and a grunt, Mika changed his tone and turned back to Takayo again with a smile.

"Okay, a conversation for another time. Now, about the boy. I can see the need for you to get to him. You have a sense of duty. And I have that same need, but we must keep our heads about us. We can't simply charge the palace. What do you have to say about it, Master Kon?"

Master Kon stepped forward, rubbing his chin. "It seems clear that we either get the Shinto-Kamie to attack the palace or use one of my tunnels to sneak back inside."

"It seems clear to me, Master Kon," Mika said, rubbing at his side, which looked almost healed now, "we must do both."

7

It took them ages to get back to the port, walking along the beach, but when Takayo saw Jon get on the new Shinto-Kamie ship docked there, she couldn't stop herself. She began to weep.

"Now don't fret, Waterbringer. He will be safe. Far safer than we will be, I assure you. He is the best one to deliver our plan to Master Chi'en. For now, we must go. We have much ground to cover and not a lot of time."

Takayo turned from the sight, wiping tears from her cheek. A stream of moisture smeared across her pale chin before turning cold in the blistering coastal wind. She stomped away as the man-of-war swayed behind them, its large sails snapping in the wind.

"Takayo?" Mika said after a time of walking.

"Yes."

"I'm curious... I have a notion about that blade of yours. Would you mind forming the blade and letting me look at it?"

Honestly, Takayo didn't know if she could. She had only formed it once, and that was when Master Kon had startled her. She grabbed the hilt in her pocket and attempted to harness that feeling of defensive surprise. She held out the hilt and was suddenly aware that she could force water through and out the hilt. The blade instantly erupted and froze before them.

"Don't let it go," Mika said, grasping her wrist. He looked the blade over and noticed an inscription on the ice of the blade. "There are words here, Takayo."

She hadn't noticed that before and moved the blade closer to her face.

That which was once dead will rise.

That which was once lost will be found.

That which was broken will become whole.

"**W**ords of the Dragon King," Mika told her. "A Dragon King Prophecy."

Takayo fingered the hilt, and after a time, a feeling odd and unfamiliar crept up inside her, like hearing her name whispered in a crowd. The words swam at her, soft and distant.

Waterbringer…

She released the hilt and spun around, her eyes searching left and right, from the cold, snow-covered mountains to the crashing waves of the Black Water Sea. But she saw nothing.

"What is it?" asked Mika, noticing her sudden distraction.

"What? Oh, I just… never mind. I'm just hearing things."

Master Mika threw Kon a concerned glance in response to her comment.

The long trek from the port to the White Palace would take days to cross on foot—a trip Takayo wasn't looking forward to. She couldn't see how it could be done in time before the Empress killed the boy.

"This doesn't make sense to me, Master," she said after an hour of trudging through the thick brush of the Shi coastline. "How can we go on foot? Time is short, and we must make haste. Wouldn't it be faster to go by way of the Shinto-Kamie ship?"

"Shhh. Lower your voice, Takayo. There are ears on us," Master Kon said in an almost whisper voice.

"What?"

"Be quiet, Takayo, and trust in me."

She did it again, she thought. She overstepped her bounds. She needed to trust and not be so eager to talk. She knew that, but lives were at risk, and they couldn't simply wander the countryside while the Soulchemist was put to death by the Empress.

After a time of moving in silence, Master Kon spoke again. "We're not simply walking, Takayo. We are *evading*."

"Evading who?" she wanted to know.

"Bushi spies. They are close. And we must rid ourselves of them first. I have a contact in the next town who will smuggle us onto one of the grain ships supplying the city. But we must be careful. Eyes and ears are close."

"Why don't I just—"

"No!" Master Kon snapped. "Your powers are unstable, and we can't risk it."

"Unstable? I can—"

"You can what, child? Your abilities are an uncontrollable storm lashing out this way and that."

She stomped further into the brush, keeping herself a few paces from him.

The gods chose me, Takayo thought. *How can he not see that? If the Dragon King trusted me, why not the sword you?*

"Takayo," he called to her in a hush. "Don't act like a petulant child. You may be chosen by the gods, but you are not ready."

She spun around like a top and faced him. "How did you—?"

"Like I've told you before, you wear your emotions all over your face. I read you like a scroll." Heat flushed her face.

She turned again and skulked off as his words settled in her mind. Each one had its weight that hurt her. It went on this way for some time. It wasn't until their trek took them to a forked path that led them away from the watery coastline that one said another word. It turned out to be Mika.

"Master Kon, up ahead," Mika said, pointing to a distant spot. Both Takayo and Master Kon turned to where he had indicated. It was a shimmer of light peeking through several sapling trees standing on a hillside. The rising sun was catching something metallic off in the distance. Then—in an instant—the ribbon of light was gone.

"What *was* that?" Takayo asked, pulling back to where Master Kon stood. She looked up at him, waiting for him to answer, but he didn't. "That's one of them, isn't it?"

"Yes. He is very still and silent. But it was a clumsy move for him to let his blade catch the morning sun," Kon told her.

"Or he wanted us to know he was there," Mika said, approaching them.

Master Kon watched the spot for several minutes, and the whole time he rested his hand on the curved handle of his Bushi weapon. Takayo thought that he was ready to draw it at the slightest movement. She recalled how easily he had taken out the Bushi knights in the courtyard, how skilled he was, and why he was called 'the old sword master.' Because there was no one as adept with the Shi-ken as Master Kon, she told herself. She took a deep breath and tried to remain still.

Suddenly a sword tip raked across the long blades of grass somewhere behind them, and before she could react to the cutting of air behind her, she heard a small gasp escape Mika's lips. Her hand shot to her hilt, but by the time her fingers touched it, Master Kon's sword draw was complete as he whipped his weapon out of its scabbard.

"Don't move, sword master," a man standing behind Mika spat out while holding a small blade just under Mika's throat. Takayo could hear it roughly scraping the stubble on his unshaven neck. Takayo tried to push the ice blade from her hilt, but she couldn't do it. Master Kon was right, she thought. Her power was as unpredictable as a storm. Yet there was something else; the water was calling out to her from the men. She was already connected to it. The water wanted to be free of them. It wanted to be with her. So Takayo did what she used to do to men who thought they could simply take what they wanted.

"Awhg!" the Bushi knight called out and dropped his blade. An instant, a thin red line opened across his cheek and went down his jaw into his neck. The man stumbled backward before falling to his knees with the strangest look on his face. That's when she saw the trickle of blood hanging off the tip of Master Kon's sword. She hadn't even seen the sword swing! And as smoothly as the blade was drawn, Kon's sword danced back into the onyx sheath on his hip.

Master Kon turned and shot her an angry glance.

"I helped," Takayo told him, helping Mika up.

"I told you—"

"Give it a rest, my friend. She's not going to stop now, not after all of this. And she *did* help, you know," Mika said, brushing the blood spot from his neck.

"I know, I know. She just won't listen!" he hissed.

"Did you listen at that age?" Mika asked.

"Perhaps not," Kon reluctantly confessed. Master Kon took several steps in silence before speaking again. "I don't understand. I thought they were spies reporting our movements. How does attacking us serve their purpose at all?" Master Kon asked Mika.

"They could have reported us to any noble families loyal to the Empress at either Dorr or Shi or even Carcey," Mika told him. "They may have gotten an order to kill us on sight. Things could have just gotten a lot worse for us."

"We need to get back from the water. We're too exposed here," Takayo said, looking around for anything strange to reveal more potential attackers.

"We need to get to the palace. But safely," said Kon urgently.

Hours later, as the sun fell, they came across a small, quaint fishing village on the far east bank of the outer Dorr territories. Takayo felt ragged and worn out as they rounded the last turn, and the small yellow eyes of fishing lamps peered back at them from within the denseness of fog as she had never seen before. It was thicker than the worst fog out at sea viewed from the high nest of *The Black Dog*. Without thinking, her fingers reached out before her as she slowly moved. The fog was wet and sticky. Its white and grey wisps clung to her flesh, dribbling down her arm.

Water, she thought. *Of course, it's water.*

"I'll push this back," she started to say, but Master Kon's quick grasp stopped her.

"No, it will give us cover. Bring it closer."

"What? Closer? Okay."

An instant later, the whiteness around them grew greyer and greyer. What little illumination could be seen only a moment before was now nothing more than a point of light in some far-off place. The outline of the nearby shacks and wooden homes vanished in the foggy soup.

"What now? I can't see a thing," Takayo said to where she thought the others stood.

"Take my hand. I will lead us to where we must go."

She didn't know where Kon was, but she stuck her fingers out in the general direction of his voice. He seized her fingers tightly in his—a little *too* tightly; she thought as he pulled her gently forward. She could feel the elements calling out for her when the thick fog moved past her face. It was like that now for Takayo. It didn't feel so much like she was calling out to the elements but that the elements were calling her, reminding her that they were always there, ready for her needs. She liked the thought of it. It was mutual respect, a harmonious relationship between her and the water.

The group continued down a wooden pathway, their footfalls landing gently upon the water-sodden planks. With every step, another foot of the village took shape before her.

"Master..." she began to say.

"Shh. We must move in silence," Master Kon whispered in her ear. What was this place, she wondered, that they must arrive undetected?

Shouldn't he tell me what it is if there is so much danger here? Takayo thought with some frustration.

After several moments of moving down the pathway, and after a turn this way and that, Takayo finally found herself standing before a rather unimpressive wooden door. It bore no marking that she could see. When Master Kon reached past Takayo and knocked, it seemed hardly audible to anyone.

Who could have heard a knock so slight unless they were sitting directly on the other side of the door?

The door creaked open a few inches, and the face of a rather older man filled the gap. His eyes looked alarmed at first but then softened a bit. His lips were old and cracked from the cold, yet a fire blazed behind him.

"Old friend," the strange man said, smiling a bit. "Quickly, inside."

The door opened, and the man shuffled away, letting the group in.

"I thought I might see you again, Kon," he said, latching the door behind them. The light of the small room hurt Takayo's eyes after the blindness of the fog, yet she looked around the cramped space with curiosity. There was hardly enough room for the four of them.

"Takayo, this is Mr. Kailuza—"

"Please, my dear, call me Kai," he said, shaking her hand. His eyes froze on her for some time. "You must be what all the fuss is about then?"

"I'm afraid so, Sir."

"'Kai' please, Takayo."

"Okay... Kai."

"Please warm yourself by the fire," he said kindly.

Moving closer to the hearth, she could hear Master Kon and Kai conversing like old friends. But as the heat of the fire touched her, the words pushed from her mind. The heat didn't burn her, yet she didn't like how it made her feel. She wanted water, and she wanted it right now.

What is the fire doing to me? Takayo wondered anxiously. Her eyes locked on the dancing flames. Heat and a painful sensation worked through her as Takayo stared into the fire. She was starting to sweat. Little beads of perspiration had begun to form on her brow, and she was feeling lightheaded.

"Master... I—"

Suddenly her vision blurred. "I can't..." she tried to say as she hurried back from the fire.

"Takayo, what is it?" Mika said, coming to her aid. "Are you alright, child?"

"Water... I need water."

"Quickly, move her away from the fire," she heard a muffled voice behind her say. The room was getting thick, and she had trouble fighting back an intense headache. The back of her skull and neck began to cramp and pained her intensely.

"My head hurts," she moaned. Her hands shook.

"Kai!" Master Kon asked. "Do you have water?"

"Uh... yes." He grabbed a small pitcher off a table behind him. "Here, my dear, drink this."

"No, Takayo, don't drink. But take it in," Master Kon told her, dumping the pitcher's contents over her flesh. The coldness of it cleared her mind a bit and woke her senses. It rained through her long strands of black and silvery blue hair and moved down her neck under her clothing. She found the elements within it, which fused with her own, hydrating her flesh.

"Thank you," she said, opening her eyes as her headache cleared and the throbbing in her neck and shoulders lessened. "I need to get away from the fire."

"Fire," Mika repeated the word. "The fire must have dehydrated you rapidly."

"It sure felt like it."

"How is that possible?" Kai asked, turning to Master Kon.

"That is a long tale. But first, is there someplace away from the fire and away from spying eyes that Takayo can rest?"

"Of course. My home isn't large, but if you take her to my room through that door there..." Kai pointed to a curtain hung over an entryway just behind them.

"Mika, can you assist Takayo?"

"Of course, I can. Takayo, let me help you up." Mika pulled Takayo to her feet with a grunt and slowly helped her into the next room. "Just take it easy. I'm sure your strength will return in no time."

The room at the back of Kai's home was dark, lit by a single candle. A small gold flame danced sadly at the end of a dying, ashy wick just next to a small bedroll on the floor. Before Takayo could summon the words, Mika leaned down and blew out the flame with one breath.

"Thank you," she said as she lowered herself to the bed.

"So... fire, huh?"

"I don't know what to say. Fire has never bothered me before. I don't understand," she told him, covering her eyes with her forearm.

"Oh, I think I understand. Fire is your cost."

"My what?" she moaned from under the shelter of her forearm.

"The one cost of your Reflection. It makes sense. Fire dehydrates water, so it is your *Doku*. It is your poison. You will need to be mindful of fire in the future, and you will need to be ready to take in water from your surroundings, even if it's from me."

"Don't be ridiculous."

"This is serious. If the Empress gets wind of this, you could be in real trouble."

She didn't like the thought of that, yet she knew his words were true.

"I know," she said after a time, sighing.

"Is your strength returning? Are your thoughts clearer?"

Takayo sat up on her elbows and thought about that. She thought her head felt lighter, and the headache was no longer a storm of horses racing around her skull. The muscles in her neck had loosened as well.

"Better, I think." She smiled at Mika.

"Good. Rest more. I will check on you in a bit. I don't know how long Kon is planning this thing will take. So try to get some sleep while you can."

After that, Mika backed out of the room and pulled the cloth door down behind him, giving Takayo what little privacy he could.

Takayo heard muffled voices from the next room, but she couldn't make them out. But she was confident she could listen to a concerned tone in one of them. She tossed her forearm back over her eyes and shut out the light.

8

Kanon would tell himself that fear could cut deeper than any blade, but that did not help the fear that crept up slowly in his neck. It was as much a part of his life now as the blackness that welcomed his morning, day, and night.

He had thought he knew what it meant to have fear, not to want to face a thing. But now, he knew that he had not. Who was this creature that he had called mother for so long? And what, in ash and embers, *was* she?

The voice, he told himself, *the voice was the real nightmare.*

That was the one he needed to defeat, to beat back into whatever dark realm it called home.

For two days, he had lingered in Zazen meditation, desperately hoping for inner sight, for the visions to come back. He had envisioned the small village for two days, and for two days, Kanon had taken something away from that village.

The village painted its way onto his mind the same way as before, but with one piece gone. He chopped the scene down to nothing but a field of long blades of grass and that large hulking mountain. That mountain with the snowy peak always looked back at him. Each morning he started anew, yet the fear in him kept Kanon from chopping away at those last few pieces of hillside that he needed to reach Zen. As if Zen was a person from his past, a person he couldn't face again because what he had done to them was too awful to admit, even to himself, as if Zen would judge Kanon and find his soul lacking.

The questions were always the same. Were there answers hidden in the village? And would those answers be the ones he needed or wanted? On this day of reflection, Kanon received his responses, but they didn't come to him through Zazen or meditation. They didn't came to him through chopping back scenery in his imaginary village. They came by the oddest of visitations that Kanon had ever received.

On the night in question—and it *was* night, that much Kanon seemed sure about, for the songs of birds had turned to the hoots of night owls and the sonic chirps of bats—the sky was as black as any other evening in the Hisan port. The rain fell, drumming the terracotta tile over Kanon's rooms, muffling the sounds of Mouse-mat's rumbling breathing as he slept in Kanon's side chair.

Kanon stood on his balcony, feeling the night wind upon his face, letting it work its way through his thick locks of hair, when, by chance, he heard the sound of a coin impact the stonework somewhere off in the distance. His head moved to the point of impact, and he stepped back into his room. The heat from the hearth instantly warmed his face, and instinctively Kanon sidestepped over a stack of books. His sense of the chaos of his unkempt room was improving in leaps and bounds, he told himself with some relief.

Mouse-mat's breathing grew evermore uneasy, and for a brief instant, his breathing stopped. Again Kanon heard something. The soft rubbing sound of bare feet upon stones pinged sharp pricks on the back of his neck, and even the Akita felt the need to lift its furry head off the softness of Kanon's bed and look toward the door. The sound was close, he thought, and he slowly groped for the Vakizashi short sword sitting on the stand by his bed.

Finding the scabbard, Kanon slowly drew the blade and crept for the doorway. He searched with fingers splayed out. Finding the cold brass of the handle, Kanon ripped the door open to the empty hall before him. He moved into the narrow space with a sword in hand, listening to the oddly silent walkway before him. It was quiet, uncomfortably so, he thought as he inched himself forward with the tip of the Vakizashi sword out before him.

In an instant, the wind swished around him. He felt the sudden change and leaped back, cutting the air before him with a blade swing. It sliced through the darkness before him but found nothing. Then, as if the wind meant to attack Kanon, a swirl of motion came at him, and icy fingers seized his shirt. Another hand wrenched free his sword, sending it reeling to the corner of the hall somewhere behind him. His brain fluttered with endorphins as Kanon fought the glacial grip in the darkness, but his stance was thrown off balance as the stranger spun Kanon, whipping his legs out from under him and sending him crashing to the floor. The impact was sudden and jarring, and in his blindness, his crash was far more painful than he would have thought. He tasted blood, and his skull thumped as it hit the hard floor.

"Easy, Prince," the raspy voice sounded above Kanon. A voice steaming with a calm pulled at the string of familiarity in his memory. He knew that voice.

"I have no wish to harm you again."

"Who are you?" Mouse-mat was up off the bed, coming to Kanon's aid.

"Stop where you are, boy," the strange voice said. "This is between the prince and I."

"My prince?" Mouse-mat asked from the door.

"Sit back on the bed Mouse-mat," Kanon ordered.

"Very good," the voice of the stranger sneered.

I know that voice!

Now Kanon was sure of it.

"Who are you?" he asked with a weak breath. His hands struggled to push his body up off the hall floor.

"I am Dás Kalos," the stranger said, bowing. "No, no, please don't move," the ominous stranger told him, drawing a sword. Kanon might no longer have the use of his eyes, but his ears picked that sound up quickly enough, he noted.

"What do you want?"

"To talk."

"*Talk?*" Kanon asked, pushing himself up on his elbows as his upper body cried out in pain. "I do not talk to people who break into my home and try to kill me."

"*Kill* you? Boy, I would have killed you before now if I simply wanted you dead."

That was it. The voice in the darkness no longer seemed distant to Kanon. It was the voice of a memory too difficult to face, yet he knew it in his heart.

"You!—"

"Shh... Soft voices, Prince Kanon," the man said, bringing the tip of a sword close under Kanon's chin in the darkness. And Kanon remembered that sword. He recalled the straight blade of the Chokuto sword that had taken his eyes.

"We must be quiet. I wouldn't want your guards coming after me now."

The thin edge of the weapon pushed the soft flesh of his neck again, yet did not cut Kanon.

"You took my eyes," he grunted at Dás. Kanon felt the man grow closer to him.

"They were holding you back. I took your eyes, but I gave you so much more."

"My *eyes* were holding me back? Ash and embers, what does that mean? You blinded me, you idiot! I should kill you," Kanon gritted his teeth at the sound of the man's voice next to his ear.

"By the looks of you, Prince Kanon, you couldn't kill a cat right now. You should thank me for taking that which betrayed you. Your eyes said too much to those who you keep secrets from."

"Secrets?"

"Yes, fear is a secret."

"What do you possibly know of my fears?" Kanon asked the stranger furiously.

"I know everything about you. I saw it all in those eyes I killed."

Dás drew his blade from under Kanon's neck and threaded two fingers under the bandage over Kanon's eyes, pulling back the grey cloth to reveal white eyes slashed with white scars.

"You are an excellent warrior, Prince Kanon. But the eyes gave away your every move. They told me what you were going to do before you did it. But look at you now. I took you down with the most basic of moves. I will make you into something amazing. It is all inside of you, asking me to bring it forth. And I will. I will form you, forge you like a blacksmith and hammer."

"I. Can't. See!" Kanon said, wrathfully emphasizing every word.

"Blindness is not a handicap, my boy, but a freedom. Your sight was holding you back."

"What do *you* know about it?"

"I know everything about it, Prince. Just like you, I was blinded by a blade. And just like you, I was angry at the loss of my eyes. It is the simple thinking that you must overcome now and see in a new way. You have a sight within you that you must learn to use. Anger is never without reason, Kanon. But in this life, it is anger that will see all your hopes and dreams taken from your grasp. Do not let wrath push you off your path. You still have sight. Use it now."

"What sight?" Kanon pushed the stranger away and climbed to his feet. "And why did you do this to me?"

"That is a myriad of questions, Kanon. First, let me say that I did this to help you. I did this to teach you."

"To teach me?"

"Yes. I am a Shadou-wāgu. We are members of the High Order of the Soulchemist, guards of the north. We are an Order that can be traced all the way back to the lore days of the Slave Wars. We have watched the Soulchemist for generations. And just as the Knights of Onyx fought to free the slaves from their oppressors, the Shadou-wāgu have fought to keep the Soulchemist free from eyes that wish to harm."

"The Soulchemist?" Kanon repeated the word. "I know that word."

"Yes, I know you do. To be a member of the Shadou-wāgu, you must first be a Mentalist—a Mentalist who has opened their mind, Kanon. I've watched you for some time, and you've taken the first steps into Mentalism. You saw the Empress for a little of what she is, and you heard with your sight. You saw her through your mind. In time, you can see the world around you as you have never seen it before. Soon darkness will mean nothing to you."

"Wait, wait. This is far too much information. Let's go back to the Shadou-wāgu guards. You protect the Soulchemist, the Soulsmith boy?" Kanon moved down the hall and groped for his Vakizashi blade in the shadowed ground.

"Yes."

The stranger moved in close to him and helped Kanon move away from his rooms, where he could hear the loud breathing of Mouse-mat. Kanon shook off his fingers, feeling them upon his shoulder.

"I don't want anything from you. Get out of my house!"

Dás moved faster—faster than before—and sent Kanon reeling into a guard rail between staircases. His ribs racked the ironwork of it, and Kanon fell to his knees in pain. The young man wrapped an arm around the railing, attempting to hold his body up.

"You are in danger, Prince Kanon. The Empress wants you dead. You saw a little of what she is, and very few have lived to tell the tale of her origins, my boy. I can either be a friend to you or an enemy. It looks as if you can't handle me being an enemy. Now I offer you friendship. And it will be the only time I offer it. So which will it be?"

Kanon thought about that for a time, feeling his ribs ache and his skull thump. He thought about the truth he so desperately wanted to unravel, and something within Kanon told him that this man had truth within him. But would he share it with Kanon?

"Okay. It is friends, then." Kanon muttered savagely. The words were difficult for him to get out.

"Good," the stranger rumbled at him, pleased with his choice.

"Mmm... And you want to teach me to be, what... one of these Shadow people?" Kanon whispered, climbing to his feet and rubbing the back of his head. The two slipped around one of the corners and found a small stone seat hidden away from the walkway, out of earshot of most people who might wander by.

"I want to mentor you, to be your guide in the mind's eye. There is a sight beyond sight, my boy. First, you need to put the anger of your loss behind you and accept that you can now move forward."

"I am angry..."

"Anger is a beast that will destroy you from the inside out. Let go of your hatred of me and let go of the beast within you, for it will do you no good. Once you have your Awakening, you will see this."

Dás reached out with two fingers and touched the dead eyes in Kanon's face, two fingers on his eyes and a thumb resting upon his temple.

"To be a Mentalist is not to be a wise thinker like the scholars would have us believe, but to be a powerful mind that can find and focus on waves and fields outside the body. In the world around us, all living things produce energy fields—from the smallest insect to the largest tree, as the waves projected in the rippling of water, ringing around rocks. Being a Mentalist means that your mind can read these waves and build a picture of them. You use the proximity of others to see, understand?"

"I think so. Maybe." Kanon had no idea what the stranger said.

"You don't. Not yet. But you will soon. In Zazen, you saw through the closed door of the Empress' bed chamber. You reach a point of peace where you let go of everything around your mind. For an instant, you used your Mentalism to see. Tell me, Prince, what did you see?"

"I don't know what I saw. It didn't make any sense to me. But it wasn't what I saw so much as..."

"As what you heard, correct?"

"Yes," Kanon admitted. "What *is* she?"

"I have the answers you so desperately seek."

"So tell me, then," Kanon snapped, his brows furrowing.

"The Empress is an ancient Soulforger. So old that her origins are lost in the great text of this world. She is a Soulchemist. Soulchemists can uniquely pull off the soul to forge with."

The words hit Kanon hard.

"What?" Kanon asked, shocked. "But… she can't be that old. Soulchemists—"

"I know, but instead of taking part of her soul, she takes other souls to prolong her own. However, that isn't the worst thing the Empress has done. Soulchemists aren't overly powerful creatures. Normally they can be quite fragile. That is why my Order exists at all. Yet the Empress has great power. Why?"

Kanon couldn't help but recall the deep, growling voice he had heard speaking to the Empress. "She evoked a creature, a god of some dark power—"

Kalos interrupted the boy to explain, "The true origins of the Soulchemist can be traced back to the Slave Wars and the first Knights of Onyx, the Elemental Forgers. They were the start of it all. The Soulchemists find their powers like anyone else, with an early childhood Awakening. The dream comes to them, but while most of us are only contacted by our Reflection god, it is different for Soulchemists. It is an open door for any god to walk through. For Daku, it was the god of death. He sucked at her power in that dream so much that she nearly lost her entire soul. Then something happened—some sort of deal was struck. A deal for immortality or longevity. She promised the god of death something," Dás said with resolve.

"She promised him Soulchemists, other than her. She has already killed one," Kanon whispered next to him.

"I know. And she must not destroy the next, Kanon. We must stop her."

"How? She has already sent soldiers to the north."

"The Shadou-wāgu will protect him from the Gos. It is *you* we must be concerned with."

"Me?" Kanon asked, stunned.

"When Master Kon reached out to the Shadou-wāgu and informed me that a Mentalist was close to the Empress—"

"You know, Master Kon?" Kanon wanted to know.

"He wears many helms, your old master. But let us say that I know *of* him. It is because of him that I am here. I knew that taking your eyes would cause your mind to reach out, and combined with Master Kon's urging for your Zazen meditation, we knew a rebirth would occur."

Again anger flared inside Kanon. He hadn't recalled ever feeling used by Master Kon, yet at that moment, *exploited* was precisely how he felt.

"He used the excuse of protecting the Soulchemist to manipulate me into this whole situation?"

"It was a step that needed to happen, my boy. Do not think badly of the old sword master. I gave him little recourse. Events took him from your side, but regardless, your eyes needed to go. Your eyes—"

"I know. I know they were 'holding me back.'"

At once, a clatter of footsteps erupted on the staircase next to Kanon, sending Dás fading into the shadows on a gust of wind. Kanon climbed to his feet, reaching out with his arms and swinging around. He felt for Dás, but the stranger was gone. A single kitchen maid climbed to the top of the staircase, holding a tray of tea. She smiled politely at Kanon, her skirts softly rustling in the evening air, and then she disappeared around the corner and away from his range of hearing.

"My order and the Shinnto-Kamie Order have a tense relationship, almost as tense as the relationship that Master Kon has with them."

"What do you mean?"

"He stepped on several toes when he made a life for himself away from them. How long did it take for Master Kon to finally confide in you and tell you the truth about who he was? You knew him for most of your life by that point; is that not right?"

"Last year," Kanon told him. "He told me a year ago."

"Precisely. Because the truth that brought Master Kon to you could get him killed; if the Empress ever discovered who he was, she would most likely put your swordmaster to death."

"I know."

"Then you must also know that remaining here and training the future Bushi Gos soldiers put him on outs with his order, with his family."

"I am his family," Kanon snapped.

"There are more than one family in this world. A found family can be powerful, almost stronger than the real thing. The fact is that you were bound to Master Kon, and he to you. Yet, he chose to leave you and start you on this path. Why? Because you needed a push."

"So then, you're here to push me?"

"Right off a cliff if that is what it takes."

9

The boat was huge.

Takayo shaded her eyes from the morning sun as it rose over the deck of a massive cargo ship bound for the capital city of Hisan. Long shafts of sunlight warmed her face as she moved up to the edge of the port and waited for Mika and Kai.

"Good to see that you are rested," Mika greeted her, pulling himself to his feet.

"Are we set then?" Master Kon asked Mika while looking over at the ship.

"All set, indeed. Kai has a set of documents for the deck officer. We are only listed as cargo. He has gone ahead and will meet up with us there."

"I'm cargo?" Takayo asked. "That's it. We are just being shipped back into the city?"

"Simple works for me," Mika said.

"Okay, let's get moving then," Master Kon said, stepping away from the shelter of the silo and moving toward the ship. The ship was black and as big as a whale bursting out of the sea. Long masts rose above them with flapping sails that snapped like a whip in the morning. Voices of men unseen sounded like ghosts to Takayo as she approached hesitantly. She strolled down the dock to where two guards waited with the gangplank behind them. The men stood with swords drawn as many sailors came and went uninterrupted. Before she knew it, Takayo was in the position to be the next person to move past the guards. She caught sight of Kai standing by the guards, looking as if he belonged there.

Takayo didn't know what was to happen, yet she fingered the hilt in her pocket. The very act seemed to calm her nerves. When she touched the god weapon, it soothed her anxiety and opened her mind in a way she never could before.

As they drew close to the largest of the guards, Kai produced a handful of documents and a small satchel. Takayo was suspicious of what was in the pouch and felt grateful for it when the contents were revealed. When they drew close enough, Kai tossed the satchel to the large guard and handed the documents to the other without slowing his pace. They all moved on past the guards without so much as a cautionary glance. Takayo turned to look back at the guards, but Kai's voice stopped her.

"Just keep walking and look straight ahead."

"Where is our spot, Kai?" Master Kon questioned him.

"I have secured a corner in the grain hold for you. It will not be the most comfortable voyage; however, it will—"

"—fit our needs," Master Kon finished his thought.

"Indeed."

After an hour, Kai was gone, and the giant ship was out to sea. Takayo found herself in a somewhat secluded corner of a lumpy pile of grain and tossed her weary body on it for a moment of rest. Inside the hold, she could feel the belly of the grain ship cutting through the choppy water of the black sea as they made their way closer to the capital city. She knew that so far down in a boat that size she would surely be under the waterline and that if a breach were to occur, they would certainly be consumed by the water in minutes. Of course, that meant nothing to Takayo, but she wasn't sure about the others.

She closed her eyes and sucked in a gulp of water-air, and the pain in her sore muscles lessened a bit. Being this far out at sea positively affected Takayo, and she knew it. Releasing a long breathy sigh, Takayo let herself enjoy the first relaxing moment in some time.

"Comfortable, Waterbringer?" Master Kon said without looking in her direction.

"What? Oh... yes. I belong out at sea. I always feel so at ease far out on the black waters."

"That's because the water calls to you," Mika said. "It's in you more than anyone else, Waterbringer. Your thoughts feel calmer, and your muscles relax more because, like the orbiting moon, this is where you belong. You will always be strong, but never as strong as you can be in the water. And the more water you have to draw on, the better."

"Then we should fight the Empress out at sea," she said in jest.

"Ha, if only that were the case," Kon said, slumping down and closing his eyes beside her. She thought about what Mika had said and how the fire had deeply affected her the night before. Takayo tried to recall if, any time before last night, a fire had harmed her in such a way. It had not. Of course, she had spent most of her years out at sea where the number of water elements far outnumbered the elements of fire, so even if a torch had affected her, the amount of water in the air around her might have counteracted any consequence, she told herself. But that didn't make any sense, she thought. She was close to the water last night, and the flames nearly consumed her. The thought of it sent an uncomfortable sensation ripping through her mind.

She let the thought slip away as sleep consumed her mind, and the gentle swaying of the ship softly rocked her thoughts into darkness.

It was in that abyss, somewhere between the sleeping world and the waking one, where she encountered it. The blackness soon danced around her. In the fog of her consciousness, she discovered it, the source of the voice. A grove of distant trees looked so foreign to her. Encompassed by the onyx mist, it looked like something she had only read about—a kind of madness. Takayo moved without moving, almost drifting from one space to the next.

Yet, as Takayo neared the grove and passed the first tree, she knew this was something other than a mere dream. Something else entirely. As a nearby branch grazed her arm, she knew this was not reality but also had some spark of truth. A dead leaf had no sensation when she touched it.

On the other side of the grove, the black mist bled through the trees and brushed strands of hair away from her face, inspiring goosebumps to spring up on her flesh. There was a sound hidden within the wind as it pushed against her as if whispering in her ear. A voice swam to her with the aggressive tone of someone who spoke with irritation. A voice she recognized yet didn't know.

"Your mind is weak, child... You will be consumed."

The wind-voice echoed around her, racing past her ears, cold as winter. At once, Takayo stood at the edge of a great chasm. All she could see was darkness below her.

"Your mind will fail you, and your body shall follow."

"Who are you?" she demanded angrily of the whispering wind in the darkness at her feet.

"Who am I?" the darkness hissed back at her, and Takayo groped for the sword hilt but found none. She realized she stood at the edge of that chasm with nothing but the cloak on her back.

"I am *you*, Waterbringer."

"What do you mean, you are me? Am I going mad? Losing my wits?"

"Of course you are. Waterbringers are all mad."

This confused Takayo even further. The voice spoke of Waterbringers as if there was a collection of them and that they were all mad. But there had only been one Waterbringer before her. Yet that one *had* gone insane.

"There was only one Waterbringer," she said firmly.

"And now there is you, bringing the number to two. And since you are just as insane as the first—"

"Stop saying that!" she snapped, stomping her bare foot on the rocky edge of the chasm.

"See, Waterbringer; you are crazy. Yelling at a strange voice in your head."

Then a thought entered her mind, something someone had once said to her.

A crazy person never thinks they are crazy. In their mind, they are as sane as any of us.

"Why are you here, voice? Why are you tormenting me?"

"That's your curse to bear. Just like the first."

"What?"

"You are a Waterbringer. And with the gift of the Dragon also comes the curse of that... insanity. It will happen. Now, or—"

"Stop it!" she roared into the darkness.

"The power that the hilt possesses will consume you. The more you use the god weapon, the faster the power will take over you. Can't you feel it slowly consuming your thoughts, slowly working its way into your mind? With every step that you take into the power, can't you feel your true self slipping away?"

"No... I—"

"You know what real knowledge is, Waterbringer? Knowing the extent of one's ignorance."

With that, the black mist was gone. The abyss vanished and closed up before Takayo.

Takayo was utterly alone to think in the void of her troubled mind. Her thoughts were full of the words of what the mysterious voice had said. A sadness sat upon her now, a feeling as cold and suffocating as the deep ocean but without its renewing energy. Takayo didn't know what to do with herself now but woke.

10

In Hisan, the White Palace was not where Takayo had thought she would ever go. However, she had often dreamed of traveling. That is what had brought her to *The Black Dog* in the first place. She fantasized about sailing beyond the Black Water Sea through the Vale. But there was no way through the Vale—it was an impassable barrier on the edge of the empire, and any ship that drew near it either sank or was driven into the barren rocks.

Simultaneously, she found herself breathless at the sight of the royal architecture. She clutched at her cloak, fiddling with buttons and embroidery as she stood on the deck of that humble grain ship. When the ship rounded the southwest edge of the White Palace city and headed east, the city truly came into sight for her. It was more than she could have ever imagined. The grain ship wound around several tiny islands, turning west and east, and with each turn, Takayo kept the impressive palace tower in her field of view.

There, she told herself, *in that tower, is the Soulchemist.*

The Ashen Tower was enormous. Built upon the steep, dropped side of the Hisan Mountains, the city sprouted like mushroom caps at the tower's base and flowed to the sea's edge.

Takayo could hear the mourning of the great sea horn on the water's edge, calling for the end of the market day. The sound of it echoed from the seaport to the Ashen Tower and beyond.

"How many people live in the city, Master?" she asked without looking away from her surroundings.

"Almost one million altogether. However, only three thousand live within the gates of the palace."

Master Kon and Mika stood behind her, waiting for Takayo to step away from the ship's edge and head for the gangplank, the only entrance to the boat. They guessed she would be itching to see the new landscape before them. However, it took some encouragement on Mika's part to pry her away.

"Please, child... the next part of our journey awaits. We must get below, away from the eyes of those who would tell our tale. The Shinto-Kamie have many enemies here, and I would hate for all our trouble to be for nothing."

"Fine," Takayo sighed in resignation.

She reluctantly removed herself from the deck, but just as she went to turn down the stairs to the belly of the craft, the ship took its last turn around the final island and came within sight of the ports. It was there she spied it. The collision alarm sounded at once, and a cannon blast ripped across the grain ship's bow.

"Contact!" the call came from high in the crow's nest. The three of them raced back to the railing to see a fleet of warships had taken up positions around the entry to the ports. Each one seemed more significant than the next. Their anchor chains were tight, entrenching them in the waters.

"Ash and embers!" Mika wheezed out. "Must be the whole fleet! We're sunk."

Takayo reached for her hilt, but Master Kon gripped her arm tight.

"No. There are too many of them."

"What else are we to do, Master? The grain ship has no defenses. They will sink us without even thinking. Word must have reached them somehow that we were coming."

For a moment, he would not reply. It seemed to Takayo that Master Kon was thinking for far longer than was necessary. Finally, he turned and answered.

"No, Takayo. We cannot fight. Mika and I will certainly be killed in the process. The Empress, by now, will be aware of your Reflection. Word must have reached her from the Bushi you fought in the square, not to mention the assassins you killed. But she may not know the extent of your abilities. I suggest we let ourselves be taken."

"What? No, Master! Not after all of this. We've come so far!"

"They will take us to the palace holding cells under the Ashen Tower, just where we want to be. We must adapt to the situation, Takayo. Our plan to sneak in is dead; adapt and overcome."

"Kon," Mika said warningly, "they may just kill us on the port as an example."

"I don't think so, my friend. The Empress will want to talk to us. She will make it personal now."

"What of my hilt, Master? I can't lose it. I won't!"

"Give it to me, child," Mika said, shooting his hand at her. "I know what to do."

"You will stay here then?" Master Kon turned to his old friend, seeming to know what Mika planned to do.

"Yes."

"You will play as one of the sailors of the ship?"

"I've done things like that before," Mika said flatly.

"Yes, but sneaking past one blockade of soldiers is very different from evading the entire imperial navy."

"They will most likely tow the grain ship into the shipyard under guard and question the crew before releasing them. I will simply slip into the lower labor crew. The labor crew is full of faces unknown to the upper crew. I will keep this artifact safe. I promise you, child."

Takayo glanced over at Master Kon for a moment. With a look in his eye that told her, *Yes, you can trust him*, Kon encouraged her to place the god weapon in Mika's hands. She was half-afraid that she would never see it again and half-afraid that she might never see Mika again.

The old master slipped the hilt into the lining of his cloak and ran down below, out of sight. She was about to ask another question when a cannonball splashed closer to the hull.

"We need to make it look like we are attacking them. Make a huge fuss about getting off the ship. Can you attack one of those smaller ships without using too much ability? No water-flying or anything like that?"

"I don't think I can water-fly without the hilt, Master, but I can jump over—"

"No jumping either. Let's keep it to dehydrating their minds and a little water-fighting. Remember what I taught you about the sword draw?"

"I do."

"And your black powder?"

"I have it. Once I'm wet, it won't be much use."

"Understood. Then go off the side and let them see you."

"What about you, Master?" she asked, worry tinging her voice.

"I will wait for one of their ships to pull alongside, then take out as many as I can before surrendering."

"What if they simply kill you and not take you back as a prisoner?" Takayo wanted to know.

"The Empress will want me alive."

"Really?"

"Yes. If only to torture me. She enjoys that. Now go."

As Takayo turned and leaped off the port side, she heard the booming tones of the fleet calling for her to stop. She hit the sea with a resounding splash, and the water immediately affected her, which she expected. Her mind woke, and the elements around her came to life, thrusting her forward at a fantastic rate.

Water rushed past her ears in a *whoosh* as she came upon the first hull in the fleet. It sat shallower in the water, unlike the enormous warships that sat deeper, so Takayo knew this was the ship for her. She made the elements push her even faster as she sprang forward and out of the water.

She exploded from the surface of the water like a cannonball. Waves shot upward in a spray of white mist as her body raced skyward.

But not too high up, she told herself as her body soared past the railing and she saw the crow's nest coming closer. She cut off the elements and fell to the wet deck of the Bushi schooner. Her feet landed with a slap in the middle of several Bushi soldiers who jumped backward at her impact.

"Stop!" one of them yelled, shocked.

She jerked her blade from the sheath and cut the air before her.

Make it look good, girl, she mentally whispered to herself.

Takayo knew that her sword skills were no match for one of the Empress' Bushi knights or seven of them. They lunged at her in unison, and instantly the water within their tissue sent their bodies tumbling backward.

Too much, she thought. But she went with the flow, jumping forward and coming down with the full weight of her Shi-ken upon the first man's armor. Takayo spun off the soldier finding the elements within the following attacking soldiers, and sucked the water from their muscles, sending the men to their knees in pain.

Suddenly arrows dropped from the sky and drummed the deck around Takayo. The *thock, thock* of arrows splintered the wood around her. Takayo spun at the sight of numerous ships coming into range as a volley of arrows rained down from above again and again.

She ran as fast as she could for the closest cabin doors. Arrows cluttered the decking behind her as she ran, whipping close to her face. It swung open just before she reached the door, and several more men filled the doorway. Takayo shouldered into the men, and one of them seized her shoulder with a mighty grasp. Pain shot through her momentarily.

"Agh!" she cried out.

"I will break every bone in your body!"

She spun around clumsily, grasping for her flintlock. She wrenched back on the gun's hammer, but it slammed down on wet powder. In a frantic attempt to free herself, Takayo jabbed the weapon out, striking the man on the bridge of his nose, which sent him stumbling.

"Oh, no, you don't, girl!" another soldier said, backhanding her with a mail glove across the face. She tasted blood. Anger shot through her, and the man flew through the doorway from which he had come. The fall shattered his forearms and sent him back down the wooden stairwell before he stopped on some barrels of black powder at the bottom of the stairs.

"That hurt," Takayo said ferociously as she jumped for cover. More arrows shot around her, one nearly taking her in the neck. She turned to spy on Master Kon on one of the other ships. Dozens of bodies lay before him, but he gave up his sword to the Bushi just the same.

Must be enough, she thought as another group of large Bushi ran up the stairs. They practically filled the doorway, some with swords and some with flintlocks, all pointed at her. She knew defeating them would be an easy task. Yet, just the same, she dropped to her knees and tossed her sword at the foot of the nearest man.

"I surrender!" Takayo yelled for all to hear. The Bushi swarmed her like a pack of wild dogs, throwing her to the wet deck. The kicks hit her chest and ribs hard, knocking the air from her lungs. She choked and gasped for breath. She was already lightheaded, so when the powerful kick to her skull came, she could do nothing about it.

The world went black.

When Takayo woke again, she found herself in shackles. Her feet dragged along the cobblestones and felt bloody. It hurt to open her eyes, but when she did, she saw the city gates open wide, like a mouth of wrought iron. Several Bushi dragged her through the opening. They stank of musk and wine, their grip fierce and unrelenting, like nothing Takayo had suffered before.

"Takayo," the weakened voice of Master Kon spoke to her from behind her. "Takayo, are you alright?"

"Yes... I think so." But her head hurt badly. "Are those the main gates?"

"Yes."

The two prisoners were dragged up to the gates by several prominent Bushi soldiers. One of the knights held Takayo under one of her arms, wrenching her shoulder so hard she swore that her shoulder might tear clean off.

"First time at the palace?" Master Kon asked softly.

"Y...yes," she stumbled over the word.

"The first time you see it... well, 'breathtaking' is the word commonly used."

"Yes, breathtaking," Takayo said, smiling at the irony. Her bruised lungs certainly did make it difficult to breathe.

"The palace is part of one of the empire's most sheltered, protected major cities. It was built upon the ruins of Tranquist, the lost city of the gods. The destruction of that ancient city carved the Hisan Mountain Range into this giant cliff where the tower now stands."

"Silence, traitor!" one of the Bushi yelled, elbowing Master Kon in the side of the head.

She couldn't help but visualize a god city grander than the Ashen Palace. She tried to see the mountains as they would have been a thousand years ago and how much water it would have taken to destroy something so huge. Standing at its base, she felt like an insignificant ant looking at a whole universe ready to kill her at any moment. Ready to erase her forever.

As the group stomped down and clattered over cobblestones, clomping gruffly down narrow alleys and up roads that twisted like a river stream, Takayo caught sight of the walls of a growing village. They grew skyward before her in great stones of gold and brown, rocks as big as her head. The walls grew taller with every step she took, and a feeling of confinement consumed her. Every stomp of the Bushi armored footfalls around her felt like a sentence that was soon to unfold.

Pain slapped her shoulder when her body hit the hard surface of the cell floor. But there was something else too. Water. Takayo lay in a puddle of water. Were these Gos the stupidest Bushi in the entire Empire of Hisan? Then everything went black.

She remembered it all.

Takayo remembered the light. She had seen it briefly before they had shut her in that cold, dank place. It was only a quick glimpse, a brief spy of light that shoved its way into the darkness, catching tiny dust fragments in its yellow-white beam. Now there was only gloomy obscurity and the sound of breathing.

Her hand stretched out into the complete darkness. Her fingers found the cold stone wall and then the wet floor. Her leg pained her greatly, and with every movement, her nerves sent a tingle racing up her limbs, telling the story of poor circulation—a story of too much time spent sitting on the hard, wet ground.

"Master?" she asked into the darkness. "Are you there?"

There was no answer. Takayo could hear the breathing of someone nearby. She could feel the elements of water within a person as well. And if she could feel their water, she knew the person was not a Reflection, not Master Kon.

"Is someone there?" she asked in as scared a tone as she could muster up. "Please talk to me."

"He won't be answer'n you, girl," the aged voice said with a thick northern accent. It sounded like it came from behind a door.

"He has no tongue to speak of. The Empress had it cut out years ago. I would expect far worse be happen'n to your Master 'bout now."

"Please... who are you?"

"Who am I?" the man said. "I be your death, girl! Just waiting on da order. Not long now, I be guess'n. The Kamie meet my blade soon enough."

"What are you doing with him?" she snapped out, tugging on chains that held her to the floor.

"You have your worries. The Empress be hurt'n him. Soon she will be hurt'n you too, girl. Then I will be taken your head. I will—"

The cruel voice was cut short in an instant. Takayo had had enough of him. She heard a few last guttural moans and what sounded like his hand clawing before the loud thud of his body landing upon the hard ground outside the door met her satisfied ears.

Water misted and bled through the cracks in the door and between the old hinges as the elements ran to Takayo's flesh. When the water touched her, she was awoken. And for a moment, she could see a little clearer and hear a bit farther down the hall of her cell. After a while, the effect faded from her eyes and ears.

There were several pools of water on the ground. She thirstily took in the water, filtering out any filth, and looked around the room again. From what she could tell in the dark, it was a small room, no more than fifteen feet by fifteen feet. Her chains didn't look too large, but they were large enough to hold her. None of her abilities gave her any strength that might break her bonds. She was just as trapped in that place as she had been a few moments ago.

"Fattoheddo!" the voice came from outside the cell's darkness. "Wake up, Fattoheddo!"

At once, a shaft of light erupted into the room, and Takayo tried to shelter her eyes, but the chains binding her wrists prevented it. Suddenly a body, large and stocky, filled the space of the open doorway.

"I should kill you for this, Kamie," the man said, pointing to the body of the guard lying still on the floor behind him. He slowly withdrew his long blade from a scabbard at his hip and, with the help of another guard, pulled what looked to be Master Kon into the prison room.

Kon was barely recognizable as the man Takayo knew, his face beaten so severely that one of his eyes had wholly swollen closed and his jaw bruised to the point of fracture. The two men dragged him through the cell door, each holding onto Master Kon's shoulders. They dropped him roughly on the wet floor before Takayo's bare feet.

"M...Master?" Takayo tried to say, staring at him. Worry and sadness flowed into her as she looked at the man who had always seemed fierce and strong. Her eyes shot up to the two soldiers standing before her. "I will kill you for this."

"Make a move, little girl, and I will run you through," the closest one said, pointing the tip of his Bushi blade down at her. He stared at Takayo for a very long moment, and then just as he turned to take his leave, she attacked him.

The other man had no time to react. When he moved a hand to his weapon, the soldier was covered in blood and water. A look of agony replaced the anger she had seen in his eyes only a moment before. He turned to run, but the elements within him tore the man backward. The Bushi smacked his back and skull on the hard floor just next to where Master Kon lay.

"Don't move!" she commanded.

"What is happening?" the Bushi said through clenched teeth.

"I have control over the water in your tissue. Fight me anymore, and I will tear your flesh apart. I will rip the water from your cells with such force that your body will not be able to recover. You will be annihilated."

"I...I don't want to die," he stammered.

"Understandable. If you unlock my shackles, I will spare you," she said, holding up her bound wrists.

"The Empress will kill me if—"

"And what do you think *I* will do if you don't free me this instant?" her eyes narrowed on him.

"AGGHHH!" he cried as water began to pull from the pores in his chest and face.

"Okay, okay. Just stop... Please!"

She released him, and his right hand shot into a breast pocket. He fumbled momentarily, then produced a long, thin iron key.

"Good, now unlock me."

The Bushi guard scooted and crawled on his elbows over to her, taking the lock of the shackles in his shaking grasp. The lock snapped free with a grinding clank before falling to her feet. Takayo rubbed the sore spot where the shackles had been

"Now unlock him." a moment later, the shackles holding Master Kon clicked free.

"Master! Master, are you alright?" She rolled him onto his back as gently as possible, but he cringed.

"Awwhh, I think so. No permanent damage."

"Can you walk? Or should I leave you here?"

"What? No, no. I can make it. Just help me up."

"But, Master, really…"

"Death is not a curse to be avoided… but the natural end of all life. Death is not eternal; only dishonor is. I will not die here and I will not dishonor myself by letting you go on alone."

"So," she said, lifting him, "if we're in the cells, how close to the tower are we?"

Takayo steadied him, stepping away finally. She reached down and looked at the Bushi, rubbing his temples on the floor.

"You," she said, catching his eyes. "Give me your blades."

The disheveled man looked at her momentarily and slowly reached back, jerking on the sash at his hip. The two scabbards he wore fell loose. Reluctantly, he handed them over.

"Here, Master," Takayo said, handing the blades to him. "Are you well enough?" Master Kon eyed them cautiously before excepting them.

"I may not heal as quickly as Mika, but I will be fine."

"Let's go then… But where to?" Takayo asked, excited over this small victory.

"I have an idea."

Water blew the cell door clear off the hinges, throwing it clamoring down a long dark walkway. Takayo had gathered this destructive force from the pools of smelly water around their cell floor. They didn't have any time to lose.

Takayo moved swiftly out of the confines of the darkness and into the torchlight gleaming from the walkway walls, careful not to get too close to the fire. Master Kon shuffled close behind her with his blade out and ready. When the running guards came with drawn swords, Takayo was no longer handicapped by choosing to restrict her powers. She unleashed the elements under her control, and the men were dead before they even got within a sword's swing of her, erupting into a mist of spray that tore through their flesh instantly. She didn't bother yet with grabbing up one of their curved blades. Takayo was far more effective as an Elementalist in a tight space.

"Up that way," Master Kon directed, pointing up ahead.

They soon began to move into the tower, winding through stairwells.

There was nothing else that they could do but go up. Master Kon had a contact of some kind in the tower, and the Empress was somewhere within it. Night was approaching, and with every passing minute, the temperature dropped outside. The Vale-storm that had so far been on their backs now seemed to be coming their way. Through the tower windows, she could see the storm was full of vibrant colors—reds and blues washing over the horizon. The storm contained strong winds of attacking, bulbous clouds, large and low.

"We need the Order to attack now," Takayo said as they climbed the tower stairs.

"Soon."

Takayo was only on the third or fourth step when she heard the wail. It sounded like a siren scream coming from all around.

"What is that?" she asked, looking back to Master Kon.

"We must hurry. They know we're coming. She will send every Bushi within the palace after us now."

Several doors on the upper and lower levels flung open at once, slamming against the tower stairwell's stone walls with a smashing sound that resonated through the brickwork.

"Stop!" shouted one of the many Bushi that stormed through the door. Fifteen soldiers, all in plate and mail, rushed down the steps above Takayo. Sounds of clattering armor rushing up came from behind Master Kon as Takayo blasted forward with as much water in the air as she could.

However, the air was rather dry because of the nearing Vale-storm, and the water didn't slow the assault much. So she reached out and found the water in their minds, spontaneously depleting their hydration and sending them into a fit of pain that brought them to their knees.

Screams of torment filled the room, sounding like an animal in agony. Takayo grabbed hold of the water in their tissue and flung them to the right, sending the Bushi tumbling off balance and off the edge of the stairwell out of her way. She didn't have time to kill them all. She spun around, ready to defeat the guards coming from behind, but was shocked to find they were all dead.

Blood dripped off the tip of Master Kon's weapon. His expression was one of someone calm and practiced resolve. No joy or regret was written on his brow as Takayo looked upon her master with awe. Only calm.

"Alright. Let's go then."

She stepped up the stairs, yet Master Kon did not follow. Looking back, Takayo saw a trickle of blood flowing down his leg. Before she could think to move to him, a shadow glimmered at her feet. What looked like a small stone or a hand-sized cannonball clanged and bounced down to her, thrown from the steps above.

"Explosive!" Master Kon yelled out, pushing at her.

The stairs under her shook. Flying bits of rubble consumed the small space, and the shadows around her began to wither and dance to nothing. She leaped from the stairwell to a lower section. Another explosion rocked the tower, and light consumed her vision. All at once, the heavy stone wall of the tower stairwell crumbled. She dodged to the side as several stones speared through the air where she had been standing. She ducked between them, eventually forcing herself to leap again. Takayo landed hard, and when she came up, she was limping.

Despite the pain in her leg, she dove over several fallen dead Bushi soldiers, sweating and sucking in what water she could. She looked over but saw no sign of Master Kon. She couldn't turn in all directions at once but had to keep spinning around to avoid falling stones. She paid little attention to the busy chatter coming down from one of the open doorways up above—the doorway, she assumed, the explosive had been thrown from. She was too busy trying to keep from being crushed to death by one of the colossal stones raining overhead.

"Master!" she yelled to the last place she had seen him.

At first, there was no sound, but then his trickling tones gradually found her.

"I'm... fine."

He seems remarkably close, she thought. The heaviness in her heart lifted just a bit at the sound of him.

"Are you hurt?" she asked.

"A bit. I'm afraid I'm an easy target for them now. I think the Order has begun their attack."

"I think so."

Takayo spied movement in the upper doorway where the explosive had been thrown. There was no time to think. She could sense the water in the men, but they were out of her Elemental range.

In the next section, Takayo encountered a small bucket of water sitting on the ground just behind an entrance door to the tower. She seized the bucket in her tiny fingers and dumped the contents over her shoulders and back. It rained over her, shocking Takayo through her clothes and puddling at her feet. The water awoke the elements within her. Her thoughts flooded open, and her power felt sharper.

The elements leaped to her as she leaped into the air, and the water pushed against her back and shoulders, throwing her upward. She closed the gap between the ground and the upper level in less than a second. Fractured and destroyed tower sections raced past her as she rocketed through the open doorway.

The impact was almost more than she could bear as she collided with the armored chest plate of the nearest soldier. The impact sent the Bushi soldier reeling backward, and Takayo came down upon his chest. A rough hand grabbed at her collar, clutching hold of her. Again, pain seized Takayo as she was thrown backward, and she crashed into a wall.

The man had her by the throat now. His grip was more powerful than she ever thought possible. There she felt it, a calling deep under the soldier's tissue. Takayo quickly ripped the water from the soldier, sending him clamoring backward into two other Bushi. They stumbled and fell under his weight. It only took a moment for her to find their elements, and quickly the room was full of water-air.

An explosive blast came again, and Takayo ran to the open doorway. This time it hadn't come from inside the tower. The shot had come from somewhere out at sea. The sound of the shot was familiar to Takayo, and when it came again, she knew it well.

A cannonball blast!

"Master!" she said, somewhat out of breath. "Can you hear me?"

"Yes, Takayo. Are you alright?"

"I'm fine, Master. I think someone is firing on us."

"Not on us, Takayo. On the Ashen Palace."

"Master, you have to walk?"

"I can, but there aren't many of the stairs left. I don't think I can—"

"I think I can lift you, Master. But I think the landing might be a bit..."

"Rough?"

"Yes," she admitted. "I can lift you by throwing water on you. However, I've only thrown or pushed people."

"Understood. There is no reward without risk." Takayo took as much water in the air as she could and tossed it at Master Kon.

It was not difficult to lift him through the air like she had first envisioned. But Master Kon's body flew up to her faster than she had hoped, and he landed, flattening her small frame to the wet ground, his body unintentionally scraping and pulling her long black hair.

"Awwgghh…" she moaned from underneath him.

"Well, that wasn't too bad," he joked, flattening her to the floor.

"Funny, Master. Now please get off."

"Right, sorry. I just—"

Blam!

Another cannonball smashed into the tower, throwing up debris that shot out in every direction. Takayo's ear rang as bits of rubble rained down around her. She blinked away dust and mortar, shaking her head.

"Is the Empress firing at us? Would she destroy her tower just to kill us?"

"No… I don't think it's her. The shots feel like they're blanketing the palace. It must be the Shinto-Kamie forces. Master Chi'en must be attacking."

"What? They're going to kill us too!"

"They don't know where we are," Master Kon said. "Let's go. I need to get to Kanon so we can find the Soulchemist."

11

Kanon stared with blind eyes through the closed door. Shock filled him as his mind raced. He looked through the eyes of those in the room. Could he take control of them like other Mentalists? He didn't think so.

Can I break down the door? No, there are too many guards. I would be killed at once. Can I get help? Will any of the guards follow my order to stop this? No.

There was only one person that he ever really trusted. Master Kon. But even he was nowhere to help.

At once, a cannon blast erupted beyond the hall window, blanketing the side of the building in a spray of dirt and soil. Kanon ripped his vision away from the guards and found a Bushi soldier below the tower. He entered his eyes and saw it all.

He could see there was a war raging in his homeland. A fleet of what looked to be warships had sailed into the Hisan harbor, unleashing a full broadside battery at once. All cannon decks were open and blooming with black powder. Swells of smoke spat out from every cannon's mouth and sent balls hurling toward the Ashen Palace, towards his home.

Kanon was saved from the strike by chance. While spying the ships in the distance through his stolen eyes, he moved a bit closer to them—trying to see a little better—when he stumbled over a potted tree sitting next to the window and fell backward.

Three sharp spears of fragments came shooting at him. One sliced clean through his jacket and cut a line through his flesh, missing his spine. He gasped and rolled away from the spot on the floor. He cursed and took off, running down the hall blindly. He heard the fragments again rocketing through the hall. Kanon was very quick, but this time, the angry red line in his back hindered him as he ran.

The Shinto-Kamie are coming for her, he thought. *Are they going to kill us all to get to her? Is Master Kon with them?*

Kanon knew better than most that this was a move that would eventually happen. Master Kon had spoken of it in their training seasons on more than one occasion. But this? This was far worse than anything he could have imagined.

Kanon closed the gap between the hallway and the door to his room in only moments. He closed the heavy wooden door, nearly knocking it off the hinges. He leaped across the space of his room, finding the spot where he hid his Shi-ken sword. Just then, an explosion rocked the small area of his chambers, sending him flying across the room and over one of his dressers. His body landed in a heap on the back side of his room.

Darkness consumed his mind several times as the sounds of destruction worked into his brain. Finally, after several moments, Kanon coughed, rolling over. He was on the ground. His ears rang as bits of his bed chamber floated down in the air around his face.

Ash and embers, now I'm deaf and blind! Kanon cursed.

Just then, he saw his old Master running to the stairwell from outside. The warrior ran with a young girl fast on his heels. They both took the stairs in long strides, nearly leaping, racing to the top. Kanon was intrigued at the sight of them. Kanon cut off his vision, shook his head, and pulled himself to his feet.

There was a massive hole where his window had once been—a space the size of over half the wall and a bit below it. He could feel the air moving freely through it to the smoky outside. He gaped at it momentarily, then grabbed his dusty scabbard and ran from what was left of his room.

"Come on young prince," Dás Kalos suddenly appeared before Kanon. "Take my hand."

"You?"

"Pull the anger back young prince. I am here to get you out of this mess. I cannot have you dying here."

"Fine," Kanon said, thrusting his hand out in the darkness. Dás Kalos pulled Kanon from his room and down the halls of his living quarters.

"The Shinto-Kamie Order is a gift. I always needed to get you away from the hand of the Empress, now is the chance."

"Kill any Bushi we come across."

"Of course."

12

Takayo and Master Kon reached another opening in the tower and left the stairwell, dashing out onto what looked like a battlefield.

Smoke curled in a dance, swaying like a snake from the ground. Cannon blasts smoldered, cratering the land around them.

It's fire shot, Takayo thought. Canon balls set ablaze."

This was the first glimpse that she got of what was happening. There must have been fifty battle-class ships out on the harbor. Half of them were sunk, and the other half were taking on water. All their gun doors were open and smoking.

Takayo and Master Kon made their way to the palace gardens, and she scanned the ships to find some sign of Mika or where he might be. But through the chaos of the battle, that proved an impossible task. Arrows littered the ground before her like dozens of discarded garden stakes.

Master Chi'en ran into the courtyard before them in full plate, carrying a long curved sword and a half-body shield. He swung out the rectangle iron plating of the powerful shield and sent several Bushi stumbling backward. He flowed through the air, slicing his sword through flesh like water trickling between rocks. Bodies of Bushi and Shinto cluttered every courtyard space as Takayo and Master Kon sprinted past.

"What about Master Chi'en!" Takayo said from behind.

"He can take care of himself. He's a proven warrior. We have our battle to fight. This way!" Master Kon told her as they moved through the large iron gate of the gardens.

They sprinted past large flowering plants of red and yellow, massive fruit trees, and stalks of ivy that seemed to consume all they touched. The doorway to the tower's inner chambers was unguarded yet somewhat hidden to those who didn't know what to look for. Master Kon slipped behind the trunk of a large cherry blossom tree, skirting the stones of the tall tower. This tower seemed connected to the main structure of the White Palace.

Takayo's thoughts were swimming with visions. She imagined Mika fighting on the deck of the grain ship and also wondered about Jon. Was he on one of those ships? Was he safe or dead somewhere?

She didn't want to think about him trapped in the midst of the battle outside or sinking in one of those unfortunate ships in the black sea. The storm was coming. And like all Vale-storms, it would be striking with the power of the gods and manifesting any moment.

Takayo moved in darkness briefly, walking just behind Master Kon. She watched every movement in the hall, ready to defend herself.

"The stairwell is just ahead," Master Kon said. The two of them rushed up the steps. Master Kon was taking them two at a time and didn't even see a figure running down the stairs simultaneously. Takayo jumped back a step as the two nearly collided with one another. Takayo spun off her heel and was about to unleash the water around her when the other man spoke in surprise.

"Kanon!" Master Kon said in surprise.

"Master!" the young retorted. "Is that you?"

Takayo looked at Kanon, who wore a bandage over his eyes.

"Kanon! What in the gods happened to you?" Master Kon grabbed Kanon by the shoulders and hugged him tightly. Then Master Kon held him at arm's length and looked at his blindness.

Kanon turned right and then left as if looking for something.

"I was attacked. I took a sword to the face."

"Attacked? Who attacked you?!"

"We don't have time for this!" Takayo interrupted them. "I'm sorry. I know this is very important, but we don't have time to go through it just now. People are trying to kill us."

"She's right, Master. We must stop her! Please, Master," Kanon pleaded.

"Where is the Empress?" Takayo insisted. "We have to find her before she hurts Roa."

"Let's go. Are you well enough to take us?"

"I see better than most now, Master. But the cloaked stranger, Master—he's something dark, evil... He has Roa," Kanon told him, running up the stairs.

"We will handle him, Kanon."

The three of them turned and raced up the stairs. Master Kon and Takayo followed closely behind Kanon. The Master jerked his blade free as they reached the door, as did Kanon. They stopped just short of the large, weighty door that was as tall as a giant and just as wide.

"Master, my mother always keeps several well-armored men with her. Do you think we can—?"

"Yes. They are no match for Takayo Jin here."

Takayo took that as an introduction. So she gave a clumsy side bow to Kanon.

"Master, I don't see how—" Kanon started.

"Trust me. Takayo, ready? Can you sense the water within them?"

Takayo closed her eyes and instantly found the water on the other side of the large door. "Ready, Master. There are six of them. Two by the door, two by the window in the back, and two in the center of the room, though it is harder for me to sense their elements."

"That will be the Empress and the Soulchemist."

That was all Takayo needed to hear.

She was finally here, and she wasn't going to fail now. Rage built within her—a need to finally make things right. She couldn't fail now. She *wouldn't* fail now. All the events had come to this.

Takayo sucked in all the water-air that she could and unleashed a massive tidal force upon the iron door of the chamber. The door tore from the hinges and tumbled into the room's darkness, nearly crushing one of the Bushi soldiers under its weight. The three of them flooded through the doorway, and Master Kon and Kanon moved onto the soldier at the front. Kanon confused the soldier with a force of Mentalism as he ran blindly toward him.

The Empress held Roa dangling above a pool of red flames. A strange-looking blade clutched in her fingers. The boy looked weak as if his life was quickly fading away.

Are we too late?

A substantial red flame surrounded the Empress and the Soulchemist in the chamber's center. There was something else Takayo saw as well, but she couldn't form the thought in her mind. A dark red energy cloud swirled between the Empress and the boy, but at the same time, Takayo was sure she could see a form within the cloud. And eyes—fiery yellow eyes. There was something unnatural there.

In a moment, Takayo was on the guards by the window. She danced between their clumsy attacks and pulled the water from their bodies, leaving them a moaning lump on the floor.

Takayo twisted and darted straight for the Empress, but movement sprang out from several directions, and a fist sunk into Takayo's lip, sending her reeling across the room. Smoke flew overhead, snaking around her. The Knight of Onyx materialized before her in a blast of black mist. His burnt fingers reached out past gray bandages, and a sword of crystal formed out of the light that nearly reached the floor.

"What is this?" Takayo asked, scrambling to her feet, tasting blood.

"I am a Knight of the ancient Order of Onyx," the man spoke, hissing at her. His massive blade cut the space between them. Takayo leaped back out of the reach of the enormous cystine blade. There was no water to take from the Knight of Onyx; one hit from that blade would be the end for her, and she knew it.

He sneered at her, "The borrowed power of a dead god is nothing to a Knight of Onyx."

Suddenly, shadows came to life around her, and elements took shape. Flesh and armor materialized before her eyes, and at once, the familiar form of Master Chi'en stared back at her for a moment. She stood shocked at his movements and the tremendous flow of elements that danced around him. He instantly closed the gap between himself and the Knight as a long sword formed in his fingers. Their blades came down in an impressive storm of clanging, thunderous metal. As Master Chi'en and the Knight of Onyx fought, Takayo clambered free of them and moved upon Daku.

There is something wrong.

As Takayo moved to grab the elements within the older woman, she was shocked to find that the ancient Empress had none to manipulate. She was a Reflection or something.

Who doesn't have water within their body? she thought, stunned. She moved in closer but was overcome with weakness. Panic rose inside Takayo the closer she drew to the flames.

Fire. I need water. I need to take in more water.

Takayo was too close to the fire, and she could feel it affecting her cells, rapidly dehydrating her. Her mind spun, and the room shifted.

She didn't see it happen, but the cloaked stranger and Master Chi'en had vanished into a mix of elemental magic and smoke that danced about the room. Then just as suddenly, on the other side of the room, Master Chi'en reappeared behind Daku with his blade in hand.

Takayo stumbled backward at the fantastic speed of the old Kamie Master, and Kon pulled her out of the way. She was only somewhat aware of Kanon in the back of the room. He was fighting one of the guards.

"Master, what is he?" she barely had time to ask as a vast, hulking, smoky figure erupted from the fire, knocking Roa to the ground at its feet.

Takayo had never seen a sight quite like this before. Smoke curled around the black warrior. His flesh was not truly there, she thought. His hands were more like talons than fingers, black mist than solid flesh. And when the man standing in the fire drew the long black sword from its scabbard, Takayo barely had time to react.

Takayo moved her attention out of the windows. The sea air was very close. To everyone's shock, a large mist of water galloped through the open windows, bleeding between large stone pillars and dancing between statues like a stampede of wild stallions.

The massive warrior of smoke cut down fast, jamming the tip of his black blade partway into Roa's shoulder. The boy's blood spilled large drops onto the blade and into the pool of blood at his feet. The odd-looking smoke soaked into the blood and tangled between Master Chi'en and Roa. Master Chi'en seized Roa by the arm and, with a mighty pull, ripped the boy from the demon's clutches. Master Chi'en swung around, spinning his arms out, and forged a long trident from the elements around him. Chi'en lunged with his trident spear. Daku ducked just under the blow and somehow rammed the point of her blade under one of the armor plates on his hip.

A tidal force of water smashed into the center of the room, sending the Empress, Master Chi'en, and Roa sliding out of the blood and washing across the floor. The strange demonic beast had suddenly vanished in the chaos, and Takayo didn't see where it went. The remains of the fire hissed and smoked out as Takayo lifted the water back off the ground, massing it into a big ball. Then she brought it back down upon the Empress.

The impact fractured the floor, and a deep fissure in the rock webbed out in several different directions. Takayo ran to Roa and dragged his still body to the other side of the room where Master Chi'en was climbing to his feet. A thick blood trail streamed across the stone floor, and Takayo had trouble separating in her mind what was the Soulchemist's blood and what was not.

Master Chi'en took Roa in his arms.

"My boy, my sweet boy. Open your eyes," Chi'en said, holding the boy's face close. There was something there when Master Chi'en looked at the boy.

Takayo looked over at the two of them, shocked, and then over to Master Kon. He was moving to where the Empress lay. Just then, Daku's body came to life, and her blade abruptly moved with astonishing speed. Blood spat out as her weapon danced in suddenly youthful fingers.

"No!" Takayo screamed and ran to her Master.

At that moment, Kanon turned just in time to sense that the blood was coming not from her curved knife but from Master Kon's throat. The Empress moved like a cat, leaping for the window. And then she was gone. Takayo and Kanon sprinted to Master Kon, who had slumped on the floor, blood spilling from a massive cut just above his collarbone.

"S...she moved so fast," Master Kon tried to say as Kanon took him in his arms. "How could she move so fast?"

"Shh... Master, don't speak," Kanon said to his old friend and teacher, cradling Kon's head. Takayo was on her knees, hands over her face as she sat beside them. Tears worked their way through her fingers and down her cheeks. Master Kon lifted a hand and took her small fingers in his.

"The seedling has become a flower," he said. "Make your mark Takayo. Do not be forgotten."

"No, Master, I will remember you. I still need you. We both need you," she sobbed. What good is a disgraced swordmaster to the Waterbringer? You need a true teacher."

"You are a true teacher, Master," Takayo pleaded with him. "I need you."

"No, you don't. Find Mika and get the boy to safety."

Master Kon looked over at Kanon and then back to Takayo.

"I'm proud of you both—no sadness for me. Life and death are one. And I will soon be one with the universe."

His eyes slid shut, and his grip upon Takayo's fingers loosened. His hand fell to the floor, and Master Kon was gone.

Hours later, Takayo sat upon Kanon's bed and looked out onto the Hisan harbor. It was a bleak, cold morning, and the black sea was leaden with the massive tombs of half-sunken ships and smoldering buildings. The storm came closer with each passing moment, flashing color on the horizon, telling Takayo that the gods were angry with her. She was devastated by the tragedy she had allowed to happen.

Behind her on the bed, the rhythmic melody of lungs blew like a gentle breeze, swaying back and forth as Roa slept, unconscious after his ordeal. The boy looked so small and fragile. He was not much younger than Jon, but at that moment, he seemed like he was made of glass. Takayo would not leave his side. She felt that she had failed him and failed Master Kon. She hated her part in all of this. And a part of Takayo now wished that she had died on the deck of *The Black Dog* like she was supposed to. She did this. She brought Roa to this end. The tears came, and there wasn't a thing Takayo could do to stop them.

"Loss is a horrible thing, my dear," the voice of Master Chi'en sounded from behind her. "The most perfect person I have ever known is someone who knew defeat and knew suffering and loss, and he still found his way out of the depths to us. We should all strive to be just like Kon, a child. He was the best of us."

"He was here because of you," Takayo turned to him. "He was here to help you, and you still condemned him; you made him an outcast. You could have come here yourself. With your power, you could have come for Kanon whenever you wanted, but you didn't. You sent in your friend to live in the dragon's den."

"Kon loved Kanon like a son. There is nothing like a father's love," Master Chi'en said and looked over at Roa asleep on the bed. At that moment, she knew it. She knew it all.

"You're his father. You're a Soulchemist. Is everything about you a lie? You cut off all your hair, so we cannot see your true Reflections. So no one will know what you are." Takayo balled up her hands, and she wanted to pound them into this man's face.

"I'm an Elemental-Forger. But yes, I'm his father. But the boy thinks I'm dead, and maybe—just maybe—it is better that way."

"How could this happen? I thought the Empress killed Roa's father. Isn't that how all of this began? You should be dead."

"I became one with the elements long ago, Takayo. I am dead, and then I am not. I am a Forger and forged my body back after my death. These are things that are unknown to the Order. Only Master Kon knew of my link to the boy."

"What was that man in black? The smoke demon?" Kanon asked from the doorway. "You know, don't you?"

Master Chi'en turned to Kanon and gave an odd smile to him.

"I do, my Prince. He is a Knight of Onyx. Until now, I never thought I would see another one."

"What is a Knight of Onyx?" asked Takayo.

"The Knights of Onyx first appeared during the Slave Wars almost nine hundred years ago. The first Knights were Elemental-Forgers, such as myself. They forged their own blades and armor. But later, Elemental-Forgers became blades bound with other Forgers. A living spirit."

"Living spirits?" Kanon asked.

"Have you ever heard the term, '*Respect the spirit of the sword*'?"

"Of course. It is one of the fundamental rules of the Bushi."

"The Knights are the descendants of the Elemental-Forgers?" Takayo asked, coming closer to Chi'en.

"They are."

"And that's why the Knight formed out of nothing? Because he is an Elemental-Forger?" Kanon wanted to know.

"He's more than an Elemental-Forger, Prince. The Knights of Onyx were formed to fight in the Slave Wars, to fight for the uprising. The first Elemental-Forger Knights chose to fight. Now, the Knights enslave their weapons. And are enslaved by them. They are warriors of the Darkness."

"What is the Darkness?" Kanon questioned him.

"That was the Darkness," Master Chi'en said. "As much as has ever been seen, anyway. No one really knows what the Darkness is. I think you should ask her," he said, pointing over at Takayo. "She is our direct link to the gods."

"Me?" Takayo squeaked out.

"As best as I can tell, the Darkness is a god. A god killed in the wars. And not a good one either."

"So what happened to you then, Master? How did you become the father of a Soulchemist?" Takayo asked with a stern tone. She was suddenly angry toward someone she once respected, which surprised her slightly.

"I fell in love, truth be told, with his mother," Master Chi'en said, looking over at Roa asleep in the bed. And she spied a look in him that she hadn't seen before. It was the look of someone in great pain.

"I forged myself into human form and became the first of the Soulchemists."

"You mated with Roa's mother, and your elemental power became the family curse that you passed down to him?" Takayo surmised.

"I did."

Master Chi'en moved over to Roa and laid a hand on his cheek. "How is the boy?"

"He hasn't woken since it happened. I don't know if he ever will."

"The Darkness has infected him," Master Chi'en told them, kneeling down to his son. "Only the love and affection of someone close to him can pull him back to us now... I fear that person is not me. We have been apart for too long."

"How is it that you did not die if you took human form when the Empress took your life all those years ago?" Kanon asked.

"I had the choice. Die and go into the Vale or become what I once was... I chose to become the ancient forger that I once was to watch over Roa as best I could."

Master Chi'en stood back, and light danced before him as his fingers worked at something. Takayo and Kanon moved around as the forging occurred near the room's center.

"What are you doing?" Kanon asked, a little stunned.

"I may not be the one that brings Roa back to the light, but perhaps someone else can do that task for me. Someone from his past."

Just then, elements formed the elegant yet weathered features of Lady Cobalt, the Shadou-wāgu warrior that gave her life to save Roa. She stood, somewhat disoriented, looking at Kanon and Takayo, who stared at the woman with vibrant hair and blind eyes.

"What is this?"

"I've brought you back from death, my child," said Master Chi'en. He gave her a gentle, calming smile. She may have been blind, but he knew she saw him well enough.

Lady Cobalt looked around the room with her mental vision, spying Roa asleep on the bed.

"Roa!?" she pushed past Takayo and went to his side. "What happened to him?"

"The worst, I fear, Lady Cobalt," Master Chi'en told her. "We all worked to stop this, but I fear this was a moment unstoppable. The Darkness was going to get his fingers in the boy regardless. I need you to help him if you can."

"What do you see me doing?" she looked in his direction fiercely.

"Try to reach him. Bring him back to us. The Darkness has a grip on him. I'm praying to the gods that your grip upon him may be stronger than his."

"We don't even know what the Darkness *is*," Cobalt said. "How can we help him if we don't even know what we're facing?"

"I faced what has taken hold of Daku... It is an evil that has taken over her body. An old evil crawled into her from the depth of the chasm. Kanon is the ruler of the Palace now. So Roa is safe for the moment. But the Empress is still out there and has plans for him. She is powerful. And based on what I fought in there, more powerful than any of us thought."

"She's a Reflection," Takayo finally said.

"She is," Master Chi'en admitted.

"My powers don't work on her at all. Just like how Shihan's didn't work on me."

Mika appeared from behind the doorway with a shocked look on his face. He was not expecting to see Cobalt sitting on her knees in the center of the room.

"What?! How?!" he sputtered.

Lady Cobalt turned her head up, and her lips pulled into a tight smile at Mika.

"It's a long story, Mika," Takayo told him.

"The Empress caused this damage," Mika said, grabbing Takayo's attention. "She must be stopped at all costs."

"My powers do not affect her, Mika," Takayo reluctantly admitted to him.

"That is why you need this," Mika said, pulling out Takayo's Dragon King hilt. He held it out for her. She didn't take it. Takayo watched it poised in Mika's fingers.

"I researched the hilt. It has a name."

"What is it?" Takayo asked.

"The Shard of Winter. Now take it, Takayo," Master Chi'en told her. "The gods wish it."

She reluctantly snatched up the hilt, and her flesh reacted like it had before. Her mind awoke, and she felt twice as strong. Her eyes looked brighter, and Mika couldn't contain a smile.

"Good... Good, Takayo. See? I told you the gods need you. And so do I."

She smiled uncomfortably and looked at the hilt. It *did* feel good to hold. But the loss of Master Kon was so profound upon her heart. Still, there was a part of her that wasn't hurt—an angry part of her. Very angry. She stared at the hilt, and part of her was angry and driven to stop Empress Daku, that spoke now.

"Tell me of the Empress."

Mika began, "Kanon may rule, but she is still powerful, and many Bushi remain loyal to her. We might be looking at a civil war here soon if we don't find her before it gets too—"

"That is not what she is doing," Master Chi'en broke in.

"How can you know that, Master Chi'en?" Mika said.

"The Darkness has been inside Daku for a very long time. Eons. It is what has given her immortality, but even that is beginning to fade. It is losing its grip on her. And now the Darkness is desperate. I am connected to the elements of this world. There are a trillion eyes for me to see with. The Empress is close to the Vale. She is charged with the power of the Darkness. It is ripping through her flesh. And if she gets to the Vale— You know what the Vale is, right girl?"

"Not really."

"When the world fractured, the Vale was the worst crack, and the world on the other side of that crack is the Burning Men Army, countless souls loyal to the Darkness. The gods put up the Vale to safeguard this world from the Darkness. And if the Empress gets to the Vale now...."

"She can bring down the barrier from this world to the next," Takayo said, finishing his thought.

"Disrupting the balance and plunging the world into chaos."

"I have to try," Takayo said.

Takayo moved to jump from the gaping hole in the wall of Kanon's tower, but Mika grabbed her shoulders.

"Takayo, no! I have a ship ready to take—"

"NO!" she snapped back at him. "No more death. The gods put me on this path, and I must see it done."

With that, she leaped from the top of the tower. The elements around her reacted instantly, and her body shot forward at an amazing rate, carried on water-air and a massive blast of wind. The generous elements shot up under her falling frame.

13

The long neck of the shore came and went in a blast. Takayo flew in between the long, reaching arms of smoldering shipwrecked masts, each one pushing out of the black water like surrendering flags. She rocketed close to the water's surface, leaving a spraying wake blasting out of the sea, pushing her up and forward. Seafoam pushed her flesh so hard that she tasted bile. Her hair whipped painfully, snapping at her face and shoulders. She held on tight to the Dragon King's hilt, the source of her power.

Overhead, the Vale-storm massed closer and closer. The northern horizon in her sight grew ever darker. From the low-flying line of the storm, it looked enormous, casting a vast shadow over the whole Northern Empire. Her thoughts were getting fuzzy, she noted. Most likely from the speed or the constant altitude change.

She felt like someone who was suffering from a debilitating cold. Her eyes hurt, and her mind began to get heavy. She was having trouble thinking but couldn't stop now. She didn't know she could keep to the air if she slowed her speed. It was a constant juggle between the rate she traveled and the force of the water pushing up from below her. As she neared the storm, she could see a visible point of rain and massive gales of wind at the dawn of the tempest. The fear of what she couldn't see in that storm gave her pause.

It was a Vale-storm, after all—an unknown event. Everything dealing with the Vale gave Takayo Jin pause. The massive edge of her world. The edge that she knew so little about. The edge that only gods could pass through.

Only some throughout history had ever passed through the Vale. And, once through, there was no coming back. Now Takayo was heading right for it. The shadow grew ever more significant as the continents raced by. The cold mountain ranges came and went, trapped under a cloud of darkness. Winds grew so intense that Takayo was forced to cover her face with her forearm, trusting the sea to cradle her and send her in the right direction.

Then it happened. The first Vale-storm effect. It was a colossal wave of water and rock hundreds of feet high. Thousands upon thousands of fish and sea mammals were trapped on the water's surface. But they were dead as an electrical current surged upon the water's surface.

"Ash and embers!" Takayo cursed. "I can't push off of that!"

The Vale-storm was surging with lightning clouds growing larger by the second. The wave roared closer and closer. Takayo turned hard to the left—away from the shoreline—but the swell had a long reach, and she was nearly taken out by the gust of its mass charging by her. She couldn't look back to see its path, but she heard the destruction that followed when the massive tidal wave slammed hard on the northern bank of Uenhal. The effect was devastating. It hit with such force that an enormous shard of stone on the shore was destroyed entirely. Takayo wondered if this was what gave Uenhal its odd shape. How often had the Vale-storm come to the land over the years?

The clouds grew ever darker, and the long fingers of lightning bolts shot from the darkness overhead. Vast surges of white and yellow erupted above her and blasted passed Takayo down to the water below. Several times she was forced to dodge strikes with an abrupt course change. This time there was nothing she could do. No way to fight or avoid the strike of power. No way to prevent the black, beastly cloud that had practically consumed her now. That shadow spanned the entire horizon, plunging The Black Water Sea into perpetual night.

The Vale-storm had worn away the northern edge of the land. There was nothing between her and the Vale now. Nothing but the massive power of the storm cloud. She took a deep breath. The pain in her head was forgotten as she entered the storm head-on.

It was there, just at the edge of the Vale, where she saw the warship. *The Sea Snake* was a bulky, two-hundred-gun, first-class warship. The colossal beast was half a mile out in the deepest waters, yet she could still see its wake. The Vale was as bright as the setting sun glimmering before *The Sea Snake*. Its sails cupped tight as the wind blew hard, though it seemed that, outside the storm cloud, the force was leaving the water of the Vale. All of *The Snake*'s energy sucked into the Vale like a magnet. There was a watery graveyard of sorts around the white barrier of the Vale. Dead ships' ghosts told the tale of destroyed hulls as they were pulled into the barricade.

Takayo used all the elements she could and moved low to the water as she tried to swing down to the stern of the fat warship. Takayo knew most of these massive ships had at least one chain-shot cannon on the stern, if not a whole battery of armed guns. At once, all her hopes seemed shattered when the sailor in the crow's nest gave her away and sounded the loud attack alarm. The drumming of a high-pitched bell rang in the distance, and almost immediately, a cannon blast erupted before Takayo. A cannonball rocketed past her face, and the ball nearly took her arm off. Takayo lost her focus and plunged into the depths of the waters. Almost immediately, heavy cannon shots charged down after her. Large balls of iron and lead turned the dark waters into a dance of surging, hissing bubbles zipping past her.

Takayo had no choice but to go deep, so she did. The water gave her no resistance as the elements pulled her down fast until she was so deep that no weapon known to man could reach her. Looking up, she could see the fat, wide belly of *The Sea Snake* sitting directly overhead now. The white light of the Vale was a considerable beacon that sank clear to the bottom of the sea floor and was nearly blinding her under the water. Though even in all that light, Takayo could still see the ship's shadow. Unfortunately, with so much water around her, there was no way to see how many of the Bushi might be on the deck of that ship. But a vessel of that size could easily hold a thousand men. No matter what, she was going to finish this, and she was going to stop the Empress.

Takayo held her Dragon hilt tight.

God weapons are stronger than any other weapon, she told herself, trying to bolster her bravery.

She forced the elements in the water to compel her into a powerful sea jump that would rocket her from the water's surface.

In an instant, she blasted from the churning black waves and leaped high over the ship's deck with her Dragon weapon in hand. The hilt sang to life with water and ice as a sharp jagged blade sprang from the weapon, and Takayo landed with the full force of the blade on the chest plate of a single Bushi warrior. The ice sword split his armor and mail, sending the man reeling backward as blood spilled from his body in a gush across the ship's deck. Wasting no time, Takayo grabbed the elements within one of the closest Bushi and dragged his chest to her like he was on a rope. She sank the blade into him as a flood of Bushi moved on her. The blade danced in her fingers effortlessly, and her skills surprised even her. With every swing of the Dragon hilt that Takayo took, she seemed to get better and better. With every Bushi life that she took, her skills increased. There was a part of Takayo that didn't relish taking lives, but she knew that every Bushi she left alive would be one that could snuff out her existence.

Behind her, a man came at her with a spear as long as she was. Her sword jabbed faster than she would have thought possible. In an instant, Takayo was on the soldier and finished the man off with one swing of her arm, the blade moving quickly and efficiently to take the man's life. With several dark red droplets, the water-soaked deck turned red, and the soldier was dead.

Several more Bushi came at her—not with swords drawn, but with musket pistols raised to take her life. In seconds, a chorus of explosions reported out—not from the guns but from the elements within the men who held them. The pistols clattered to the ship's deck as a sea of crimson rained down from above.

"Bushi! Kill the Reflection!" the Empress commanded from up on the top deck.

There, Takayo thought. *There she is. I will not be Forgotten!*

Takayo sucked in a lungful of water-air and erupted all the elements around her with as much force as she could muster. A circular blast mushroomed around Takayo, sending dozens of attacking Bushi tumbling feet overhead, launching many off the ship and into the black water. She swung cords of water-air like long whips, and they cracked down at the few remaining men, crushing plate and racking mail as she leaped for the wooden staircase that led up to the helm deck. Again she swung the water-air, and a thick charge of it sent the two guards of the Empress slamming into the back railing, crushing bone in an obscene crunch.

As Takayo neared the Empress, an overwhelming surge blasted from the Vale-storm. The wooden deck of *The Sea Snake* was defenseless, and the massive bolt tore through wood and tar. The ship rocked suddenly, and Takayo was thrown from the helm. She fell through the wild gusts, and her shoulder and back collided with one of the large round masts. The black sail snapped and whipped at her as she groped for a handhold. She was dazed as she looked down at the ship, trying to get her bearings. However, even though the boat looked to be tearing itself apart before her very eyes, that wasn't the worst of it. Her hands were empty.

The hilt, she thought. *I lost it.*

Her eyes swam over the ship, searching the helm where she had been tossed like a rag doll to the fore of the boat that was nearly its entity now. The vessel had been torn in two. The massive storm winds ripped at *The Sea Snake* like two strong hands pulling the ship apart. Hundreds of men were thrown from the deck, and even more, were caught in the immense drafts, tossed to their death into the Vale barrier. Suddenly Takayo spied the hilt, un-bladed and alone. It sat trapped on the ship's fore section, the part being sucked into the Vale barrier first.

The overpowering light of the barrier seemed to consume the warship before the Vale, and Takayo knew she had very little time to act. She couldn't fly without the hilt in hand—not in these winds—but, just maybe, she could catch one of the mammoth wind gusts that pushed everything toward the Vale. When a gale picked up and tore at her hair, she released her grip on the tall sail mast and tried to use whatever water-air she could gather to guide herself. Uncontrollably, she tumbled head over heels in the powerful squall.

Her vision was instantly blurred as the wind sent her flying. The white of the Vale blinded her even more. Suddenly her chest and shoulders slammed hard into a piece of the ship. The impact shook her, but Takayo wasn't caught in the overwhelming windstorm anymore. The powerful gusts seemed only to rip and pull at her up in the clouds. Down on the ship, it seemed as if Takayo had found a reprieve from the gripping fingers of the wind.

Now I am close enough, she thought. *Close enough to the hilt to use the elements within it.*

She closed her eyes and reached out. The water elements within the metal of the hilt were there. She could feel them—as if they were forged into the weapon's soul. They were close enough for her to do what she needed to do. She focused harder. The elements hadn't come to life yet. They were dormant, waiting for her command. The hilt was still too far away to move with her mind, and that section of the ship was heading ever closer to the Vale. In seconds, it would vanish along with her hopes of retrieving her one defense and one chance at victory over the Empress.

Takayo knew what she needed to do. And she didn't like the thought of it. She needed to jump into the water, but she was sure that once in the water, she would be sucked into the Vale three times as fast as any of the larger sections of the ship.

It's a risk I have to take, she told herself firmly.

The water was electrified, and Takayo thought she could use the elements within it. But she was sure that the charge of it might shock her into unconsciousness.

She jumped.

The surge was more than her exhausted teenage mind could take.

An unfathomable electrical charge ran through her body, and Takayo convulsed and fought the blackness as well as she could. It was more than her concentration could endure, and soon darkness overtook her thoughts. Her unresponsive body floated closer and closer to the Vale, passing several ripped and destroyed sections of the ship. A section of the ship luckily trapped her body called the backbone. The unit was wedged between several large rocks just to the Vale's left.

Moments later, Takayo awoke and found her body had floated up onto the long planks of wood partly out of the water. She shook the dull feeling from her mind, climbed out, and lay on her back.

The hilt.

She found it still in the section of the ship, nearly consumed by the barrier now. The elements within the weapon shot to life as she extended her fingers to it. Takayo gave a tremendous pull on the elements, and just as if she had pulled on an invisible chain, the hilt jumped into action, flying through the air and into her hands.

Instantly, her flesh grew warm, and her mind cleared. Water all around Takayo erupted upward, and her body shot skyward away from the barrier of the Vale. At once, several musket balls blasted past her face. The blade in her hands shot to life with jagged ice as another volley of lead erupted from long rifle barrels nearby. Pain seared through her shoulder as the ball in her flesh sent agony racing up her nerves once again. Several Bushi sat on a section of the helm, guarding the Empress as they neared the barrier of the Vale.

"Shoot her down like a little bird!" the Empress demanded.

Another volley of shots took to the air on a cloud of smoke, but they all went wide. Takayo closed the gap between her and the helm in one heartbeat and shot down to the deck like an arrow flying out of the sky. The Dragon sword tip sheered clean through the first man, sending him back into the Empress. The rest of the Bushi moved to guard the Empress with their armored bodies. The Elements within them erupted, and all the soldiers exploded right before the Empress, painting her now young features in a red mist. Takayo had taken the men out in the blink of an eyelid, but the Empress looked all too proud of herself for surviving the attack.

"That doesn't work so well on me, stupid child," the Empress nearly spit the words.

Anger flashed in Takayo. She dashed across the deck. Her movements were fast and determined. Takayo's feet splashed in the icy water. She leaped over shattered planks of wood, trailing water-air. She was filled with it now, fighting with it. It made her movements quicker and more robust. The elements wanted to flow through her. Takayo pushed the elements from one side to the tip of her Dragon blade.

The Empress quickly tossed Takayo's blade sideways, blocking a powerful strike from her and surprising Takayo a bit with the strength of the block. The water-air made the Dragon's blade lighter, so when the Empress moved to attack again, Takayo's blade quickly countered. The Empress shot out a stiff jab in the space between them, catching Takayo on the lip. Pain bit her and sent the girl stumbling backward. The Empress was immensely powerful, more so than Takayo had ever imagined. And as the Empress' thin blade cut the air before Takayo, she narrowly missed the edge of it dancing off her front foot.

Takayo swung her blade out, its jagged tip missing the Empress' face by a narrow margin. The Empress smiled dimly, almost smugly, at the miss. Takayo swung once more, dancing off of one foot and floating with water-air, the elements encouraging her to move more lightly.

Suddenly the Empress lunged forward, closing the space between them in a flash. The absolute agony of steel-piercing flesh seized Takayo. Her left arm was numb, hindered by the Empress' thin but strong sword. Takayo's fingers shot up to the hilt of the fine blade, clawing at the fingers of Daku. Then it was only a twist, a simple gesture by the Empress.

"AAGGHH!!!" Takayo reeled under the pain of it.

"You have caused me so much pain, little girl. It is far past time I cause you a bit of my own."

Takayo franticly kicked and swung out, desperately trying to get the Empress off her. She sucked in a gulp of water-air and found the Dragon hilt by her side. The blade sprang forward and took Daku in the shin. The Empress jerked her blade free of Takayo's arm. Takayo climbed to her feet and sucked in a massive amount of water-air, letting it fill her body with the power of the elements.

Like a cat pouncing upon prey, Takayo dashed forward in the blinding light of the Vale, spun out dancing again, and slammed her weight down on the evil, gaunt figure before her. She unleashed all the water-air she commanded and infused it into the tip of her weapon. The blade struck down with so much force that the edge of it sank clear through the Empress, its edge chopping the skeletal woman almost into two pieces as it sliced cleanly through the Empress' golden chest plate.

The chest plate fell loose, held up only by the bronze chain around the Empress' neck. Her young-looking face suddenly grew ever older with age as she collapsed to her knees. The now ancient woman looked up to Takayo and held onto the jagged section of the fixed blade stuck in her stomach.

"I was never a bad person, you know..." the Empress choked out weakly, coughing blood. "I meant... good. But power is like a drug... and I would have done anything to keep it."

Takayo withdrew her blade.

"It wasn't me, you know... it wasn't *me* that tried to kill that boy. I had too much of the Darkness in me by that point," Daku insisted.

"Every choice has a consequence. For good or for bad," Takayo said, looking down at the old woman. "You started these events eons ago. But your choices still started this, no matter what you meant to accomplish."

Daku looked up at Takayo. Her expression spoke of regret, and Takayo saw no sign of the Darkness inside the older woman when death came. No powerful surge floated out of her body like she had imagined, no dark cloud of energy. There was nothing; the Darkness was gone, perhaps returning to the Dark Chasms.

She turned away from the Empress. Takayo didn't know if the evil that Daku had taken into herself had been extinguished, but the Empress was dead.

The Vale grew incredibly brighter. Takayo spun around just in time to see the barrier had almost wholly consumed *The Sea Snake*'s helm. At once, she turned, and water shot her skyward, away from the bodies of so many vanquished enemies.

"Go. You will not be forgotten," she said to the souls she had taken.

In moments, the Vale-storm faded behind her; its fury diminished as she headed home.

But where *was* home now for Takayo? So much changed for her, so many events and mistakes, and she cannot take them back. *Can I simply go back to the Ashen Palace and call it home?* Would the Shinto-Kamie welcome her once more into their Order? Or did she now have a place in the White Palace? Would Kanon welcome her after the death of their teacher? She realized now that was all she'd ever searched for. To be welcomed. To be wanted. Had she ruined that too? Had her one chance to be welcomed slipped from her grasp?

There was only one way to find out. Takayo spun on her heels and went home.

• • • •

THE JOURNEY IS NEVER-ending.

-The last words of Master Shi-to

9 798215 886175